This book bel...

JM 12... C0-AZR-927

good book

"Do you remember where we first met?" Mercedes asked

"Sure. Salsa night at that Latino club. I asked you to dance." He trailed a lazy finger down her bare arm. "I touched you and you felt like sex."

"And then?" Her breathing quickened.

"Then I bought you a drink. A margarita."

"What did you have?"

His grin was quick and wolfish. "A tequila shot. With lime. And the salt I licked off your skin." He was getting turned on thinking about it, as was she.

"Then what happened?"

"We danced some more and went back to your place. And after that...?" His voice was rough, the way it got when he was aroused.

"We were naked and going at it the second we got to my place." Mercedes tried to glare, but it was impossible. "I'd never done anything like that before. It was crazy. Then I realized I didn't even know your name...."

He chuckled. "I remember well. I'm naked, you're naked, we're going at it like wildcats. Then you stopped and said, 'Perhaps we should introduce ourselves.'"

Dear Reader,

Most women I know are busy. I mean crazy busy. They have jobs, kids, school and charity events, they run marathons and cook dinner every night. They entertain and watch out for their aging parents and stand by their girlfriends when they break up or get sick.

These women, and by that I mean us, don't get a lot of down time. I know I don't. Two of my favorite ways to indulge myself, and take a short vacation from my life, are to read a good romance novel and go to the spa. In one day of pampering I can feel almost as good as after a week's holiday. Ah, the bliss.

So when I thought about my contribution to the miniseries FOR A GOOD TIME CALL... I decided I'd like to combine two of my favorite pastimes and write a romance novel set in a spa.

I hope you enjoy your time at Indulge as much as I have.

As always, I love to hear from readers. You can reach me on the Web at www.nancywarren.net.

Be good to yourself,

Nancy Warren

P.S. Look for my first Harlequin Superromance novel, *The Trouble with Twins,* out in December 2006. And watch for my exciting Harlequin NASCAR book, *Speed Dating,* in February 2007. Enjoy!

NANCY WARREN
Indulge

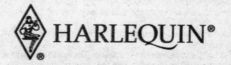

TORONTO • NEW YORK • LONDON
AMSTERDAM • PARIS • SYDNEY • HAMBURG
STOCKHOLM • ATHENS • TOKYO • MILAN • MADRID
PRAGUE • WARSAW • BUDAPEST • AUCKLAND

If you purchased this book without a cover you should be aware that this book is stolen property. It was reported as "unsold and destroyed" to the publisher, and neither the author nor the publisher has received any payment for this "stripped book."

ISBN-13: 978-0-373-79279-5
ISBN-10:   0-373-79279-4

INDULGE

Copyright © 2006 by Nancy Warren.

All rights reserved. Except for use in any review, the reproduction or utilization of this work in whole or in part in any form by any electronic, mechanical or other means, now known or hereafter invented, including xerography, photocopying and recording, or in any information storage or retrieval system, is forbidden without the written permission of the publisher, Harlequin Enterprises Limited, 225 Duncan Mill Road, Don Mills, Ontario, Canada M3B 3K9.

All characters in this book have no existence outside the imagination of the author and have no relation whatsoever to anyone bearing the same name or names. They are not even distantly inspired by any individual known or unknown to the author, and all incidents are pure invention.

This edition published by arrangement with Harlequin Books S.A.

® and TM are trademarks of the publisher. Trademarks indicated with ® are registered in the United States Patent and Trademark Office, the Canadian Trade Marks Office and in other countries.

www.eHarlequin.com

Printed in U.S.A.

ABOUT THE AUTHOR

Nancy Warren is a *USA TODAY* bestselling author of thirty romantic novels and novellas. She has won numerous awards for her writing and in 2004 was a double finalist for the prestigious RITA® Award. Nancy lives in the Pacific Northwest, where her hobbies include losing umbrellas, hiking, cooking, walking her border collie bareheaded in the rain, and classic movies. You can find her on the Web at www.nancywarren.net and blogging on Deadline Hellions.

Books by Nancy Warren

HARLEQUIN BLAZE

HARLEQUIN TEMPTATION

Don't miss any of our special offers. Write to us at the following address for information on our newest releases.

Harlequin Reader Service
U.S.: 3010 Walden Ave., P.O. Box 1325, Buffalo, NY 14269
Canadian: P.O. Box 609, Fort Erie, Ont. L2A 5X3

This book is dedicated to my editor, Birgit Davis-Todd. Every writer should be so lucky.

1

"OH, THAT FEELS SO GOOD," the woman on the bed murmured, her chest rising slightly with pleasure.

"Can you take it a little deeper?" Mercedes Estevez asked her.

"Yes," she moaned. "Oh, yes."

Mercedes pushed her fingers deeper into the skin and muscle of the woman's shoulders, chuckling at the exaggerated moaning that ensued. "You sound like you're having sex."

One eye, outlined in a deep-conditioning face mask, opened. "Honey, I never feel this good when I'm having sex. You have magic fingers, and the smell of these products is divine."

"They're made from old family recipes." A bubble of excitement rose within her. Her female ancestors had been making and sharing their creams and lotions for a hundred years, first on the family estate in Guadalajara and more recently on the family farm in California.

The women in her family kept their beauty and youthful skin far longer than nature could possibly have intended. Now it was Mercedes's dream to use those family recipes as the foundation for her own beauty empire. Estée Lauder and Helena Rubenstein were her role models; only, she was building her empire her own way. Keeping the products available only within her spa. Soon Indulge, San Francisco, the tasteful, sybaritic, luxurious day spa that was Mercedes's creation, would be running smoothly without her, and she had big plans for more spas in California, including L.A., and then she'd jump straight to Manhattan.

She had great products, a fabulous spa concept, drive, determination and boundless energy and optimism. Mercedes was going to make a success of her life, and nothing was going to get in her way.

"I don't know what I'll do if you ever leave." Mrs. Huddington sighed, as though she'd read Mercedes's mind.

Mercedes hadn't yet told any of her clients that soon she would be splitting her time between several spas and would no longer be able to keep clients of her own.

"I promise that if that day comes, I'll make sure to train my replacement so she's at least as good as I am. Maybe better."

That one eye opened again. "You're not getting bored, are you, dear?"

Mercedes smiled and told her client to lie back and relax, but she was jolted. Was it so obvious? In fact, boredom was her besetting sin. Well, one of her besetting sins. She seemed to have been beset with more than her share. It was the flip side of the ambition that made her tick.

That driving ambition married with quick boredom probably was a genetic thing. The same drive and determination had encouraged her grandparents to make the move from their native Mexico to California. Their modest farm had grown as healthily as the crops on their land. Even though her mother had married an all-American type, an insurance salesman from San Jose, Mercedes still felt a great kinship with her Mexican grandparents, spending summers picking fruit, refreshing her Spanish every year and, finally, having the family secret recipes shared with her. Not only the recipes for *sopa de flor de Calabaza* and enchiladas, but for those creams and lotions that now formed the basis of her product line.

Only her *abuela* was left now, still living on the farm. Mercedes loved it there as much as she always had, but it wasn't enough for her. She'd be bored crazy. So she took the magic ingredients growing on that land to create her spa products. And dreamed of success. Enough success to cure her once and for all of the restless boredom that boiled within her at the oddest times.

"I love challenges, that's all. You never know where I'll end up."

"Well, you're the best there is in this city. I've never felt so pampered or looked so good."

If that statement was an exaggeration, it wasn't a huge one. Maybe she didn't entirely believe her *abuela*'s assertion that the roots of her herbs had been blessed by Aztec priests. Still, she wouldn't be happy if those original plants brought from Mexico died. They were babied, propagated and nurtured with care. Indulge, Mercedes's little upstart business, the one she'd opened when she realized that she didn't have the temperament to work for somebody else, was thriving. At the five-year mark, she knew it was time to move to the next part of her plan. At moments like this one, she was overcome with a sense of pride in her accomplishment.

The treatment room was decorated in soothing blues and greens and muted terra-cotta. She'd told the decorator she wanted the feel of a Mexican courtyard. The decor was perfect, with hand-painted tiles, stone floors and a small stone fountain spilling in the corner. Her treatment beds and facial equipment came from Paris and were the best on the market. Her luxurious linens were Egyptian. Her beauty products were all natural and, apart from her own limited line, imported from Italy, though she planned to stock nothing but her own products within twenty-four months.

Mrs. Huddington said, "I probably shouldn't tell you this, but my husband loves it when I've been to your spa. He says it makes me...frisky." She spoke the last word in a whisper, and Mercedes could feel the heat of her blush under the layer of cream.

"That's good. I think it's because you relax and feel good about yourself after you've been here." She glanced down, her eyes crinkling in a smile, "I'll tell you a secret. My great-great-grandmother, in Guadalajara, was known not only for her secret creams for keeping the skin young, she also sold a special love potion."

"An aphrodisiac?"

"That's what my *abuela*, my grandmother, says."

"Do you have the recipe?"

She laughed as Mrs. Huddington tipped her head back to look at her. "What would you do with an aphrodisiac? It sounds like Mr. Huddington and you have a good marriage."

"Well, yes, but I've always wondered..."

"No. I don't have an exact recipe. And besides, I wouldn't like to fool around with people's lives that way. Though so many of my clients have told me the same thing you just told me—about how the creams make them a little frisky—that I think maybe a little of the aphrodisiac slipped into these recipes."

She continued massaging her client's neck and shoulders for the five minutes the deep-cleansing mask needed to work and then cleansed Mrs. Huddington's pores with a refreshing lotion and turned on the steamer for the next stage of the extra-rich facial for aging skin. Her movements were slow and nearly soundless since relaxation and pampering were part of the experience. Mrs. Huddington was one of her favorite clients. Every two weeks, year-round, and once a week during the hectic holiday season, the society matron faithfully came to Indulge.

"Remind me, when I leave, to pick up two extra jars of your night cream."

"Two? One should last you several months."

"I was thinking of my friend Ursula. She and her husband could use a lift. I think your cream would make a nice present."

"Don't tell her it's an aphrodisiac. It's really not."

"Of course not. I think it will refresh her skin, that's all. And I might throw in a day at the spa."

"You're a good friend."

"And you're a good saleswoman, my dear."

Her clients weren't all like Mrs. H., of course. Not everyone could give up the better part of a day "Just for myself" every couple of weeks. And that was fine. Mercedes's philosophy was that every woman—and a growing number of men—should be able to experience the utter decadence of being pampered. She had special packages for brides, for new mothers, there was her popular lunch-hour refresher and after-work wind down, which included a glass of Napa Valley wine. She could pamper a client all day, or she could have a working woman in and out in fifty minutes with time left in a lunch break to grab a quick sandwich and be back at work inside an hour.

After ninety minutes, and a few more moans of bliss, interspersed with the latest news about Mrs. Huddington's grandchildren, Mercedes turned her over to the manicurist, then slipped into her small office at the back of the spa.

Today was Monday, the day for the weekly meeting of her very exclusive women's club, the Sisters of the Booty Call. If there was a way to transform the age-old Monday-morning blahs into anticipation, she and an eclectic group of women working in the turn-of-the-century building in the financial district of San Francisco had found it.

Mercedes sat at her small desk in her small office and picked up the gray-green stone she used as a paperweight. The only personal memento in the businesslike space, she kept it as a good-luck charm and as a reminder of where she came from. That stone was from the original family estate, and every time she looked at it she remembered who she was and where she came from. She rested her fingers fleetingly on the cool stone. It was up to her now. All the family history and traditions were hers to carry on. She wasn't the first to embrace risk and dare to dream. Of course, she also dared failure, but she wasn't going to think about that. Not when she was getting ready to settle on a second location. A second Indulge.

After checking that there were no e-mails or phone messages that couldn't wait, she took off her crisp white smock and let herself quietly out the back door. She walked into the stairwell and jogged down to the main level and out into the heat and bustle of lunchtime in the financial district on a warm and sunny September day. She grabbed a salad to go at the corner deli, no garlic, since she had clients in the afternoon, and hurried back to her building, where she ran back up the stairs and entered the ladies' restroom tucked away down the hall beside her spa. In keeping with the Wentworth-Holt building's vintage, the facility also boasted a ladies' lounge.

There, among the potted plants, silk flowers, burgundy carpet, chintz upholstery and a gilded mirror, several women were sitting on a couch and matching chairs, their feet propped up on the mahogany coffee table.

"Hey," she said, when she saw Tamara Clarkson. "How's it going?"

"A'right. You?"

"Great. What are you doing here? You don't need a booty call." She widened her eyes in case one of the cutest romances she'd ever seen play out had bitten the dust and nobody had told her. "Do you?"

Tamara laughed. She barely resembled the shy young

woman with low self-esteem who'd been dragged in
here a few months earlier. "Nope. I'm still in love.
Today's a nostalgia trip. And I'll be handling the boot."

"Cool."

Mercedes munched her salad and chatted until a
group of eight women had assembled. Then Tamara
walked to the glass boot sitting on the marble vanity
under an ornate gilt mirror. "Getting ready, ladies?"

"Sure." Mercedes was never certain why she partic-
ipated in this weekly routine. It was fun, she guessed,
and a good way to hang out with the single women in
the building.

Finally Milla Page ran into the lounge. She wore her
blond hair in short, chin-length layers, and her green
eyes were deliberately smudged. She was the hippest of
them all. "Sorry, had to run down from the tenth floor."

"Don't worry about it, we haven't started yet."

Even though Milla worked for MatchMeUpOn-
line.com and so knew all the hot spots for singles, she still
enjoyed the Monday ritual. And she was a great resource
for any of the women searching for somewhere fresh to
take their dates.

"Everybody put their latest cards in here?"

"Oh, wait," said Rhonda Timmins, a paralegal from
the fourth floor. "I've got another." She dug in her purse
and pulled out a gray business card and scribbled something on the back. "Guy I met at the Wharf. Very cute.
An intense intellectual. Not my type. You know?"

They did know. That's why the boot worked so well.
The glass boot had once held a bouquet of flowers sent
to one of the women working in the building from a man

she'd recently dumped. He'd written, on the back of his business card, "Even though you gave me the boot, I hope we can stay friends." She'd laughed long and hard, and when the flowers died, she emptied the boot-shaped vase, dropped in the guy's card and said, "He's not for me, but he's a great catch. Any takers?" At least, the story went something like that. Different people told it different ways, so it had become a bit of a Wentworth-Holt myth.

The idea was novel enough that the notion of recycling men had become a tradition among the building's single female staff. There were probably a couple of hundred business cards in the glass boot of men who weren't right for some reason for one woman, but could be exactly right for another. When one of them decided to put a guy's card in the vase, she often added a little note on the back. Like, "sports fan." Or "great sense of humor, terrible dresser."

The Monday ritual was fun, and there had already been a couple of serious relationships come out of it. Recycling men was both environmentally friendly and efficient, since all the women here worked hard and didn't have a lot of time to waste on losers. It was a little like a lottery, and Mercedes couldn't help the tiny clench of excitement when her turn came. She'd met several nice men from the booty call, added more cards from men she met and hadn't clicked with. But you never knew, maybe the next one…

Rhonda deposited her new card, and Tamara stirred the contents of the boot around a bit, then presented it to Rose Leung, an accountant on seven. Rose dug into the boot and pulled out a mangy-looking card with rough edges that looked as though it had been run off on a home computer.

"Jason Thomas, Jack of All Trades," she read slowly.

Her voice was soft with a trace of a Chinese accent. She turned the card over and read aloud. "Funny, laid back. Short."

There was a quick burst of laughter. Rose was five feet on a good day. "Height shouldn't be a problem," Tamara said.

Rose tucked the card in her bag and shrugged. "If the date doesn't work out, he might need a good accountant."

Tamara passed the boot to Rhonda next who pulled a stark white rectangle. "A dentist. Cool." She flipped over the card and read, "Really nice guy. Wants to get married." She tucked it away neatly in her wallet. Then glanced up to find every woman in the room staring at her. "What?"

"Are you going to call him?"

"Yes. I'll call him."

"She's never going to call him," Mercedes said. "She never calls them."

Rhonda blushed. She was busted and she knew it. "I have to work up the courage. That's all."

"Who put the card in there?"

"Me," Tamara admitted.

"You call him. Set it up."

"No. Really. I'll call him."

Meanwhile Rose had stealthily lifted Rhonda's wallet and was already handing the card to Tamara. "Tamara's in love," she explained to Rhonda. "That makes her good luck."

Nobody ever argued with Rose about luck. She was an expert on luck. She knew the luckiest days, numbers, colors, positions of the moon and stars. She insisted it was a Chinese thing, but sometimes Mercedes wondered if she didn't have some kind of spooky gift.

Tamara promised to call the dentist and set up a date for Rhonda. Rhonda bit her thumbnail and looked miserable. Mercedes's strong mothering instinct kicked in. "You have to get back out there, Rhonda. One creep doesn't mean they're all creeps."

"I know."

"Let me know when the date is and I'll do your makeup, hair and nails for you."

She received a small smile. Finding your lover in bed with another man was hell on a woman's confidence. Rhonda hadn't dated in a year. She hoped Rose was right. Maybe the marriage-minded dentist would get their friend out of her shell.

Tamara came to Mercedes next.

With great fanfare, she dug her hand into the bowl and fished out a card.

It was an elegant rectangle of heavy stock with a bit of gold on it. Expensive. Then again so were the fees charged by the law firm of Dunford, Ross and McKay.

J. Dennis McClary was written in simple black print. She smiled a little at the coincidence. She'd put this card in the bowl herself after she and Dennis had broken up. What had she said about him? She flipped the card over and read: "Great looking. Fantastic in bed. Suit."

She was about to toss the card back in and pick again, but Milla Page was already reaching for the boot.

Okay, Mercedes thought, ignoring the strange way Rose was staring at her, she'd drawn this card for a reason. Maybe to remind herself that some men were not good for a woman. Dennis McClary was perfect for a stay-put kind of woman who wanted to give birth to the seventh generation of McClary lawyers and politicians.

For Mercedes, he was a disaster.

She was still holding the card when she returned to her office. She held the vellum rectangle between her thumb and forefinger and narrowed her eyes. Three months they'd lasted, she and Dennis, and what a wild ride it had been. Then she remembered how it had ended and her smile faded. She was about to tear the card in two when she stopped. No. Maybe it was a good idea to keep this guy front and center for a while to remind her to stay away from his type.

She tucked the card in the corner of the mirror in her office, and there it remained in the periphery of her vision as she brushed her teeth and refreshed her makeup. J. Dennis McClary.

"What does the *J* stand for," she'd asked him once when they were in bed, lazily satisfied though not quite ready for sleep.

"John," he told her. "It's my father's name. But I'm not like my father, so I dropped it to go by Dennis." He was wrong, she realized now, with the benefit of hindsight. That *J* prefaced his name for a reason. He was far too much like his stuffy politician of a father. One reason he was history.

By the time she slipped back into her white smock with the name Indulge embroidered in purple on the pocket, she looked as fresh as when she'd arrived this morning.

Before she went back out, she put her hand over the white folder on her desk, the one with the business plan she'd come up with. Okay, expanding to other locations was risky.

If she didn't try, though, if she didn't put everything she had on the line, she would never know if she had it in her to be the best.

Without guts and vision, Martha Stewart would still be offering a plate of home-baked, iced cookies to her neighbors over tea, J.Lo would have stayed Jenny on the block, and she, Mercedes Estevez, would be just another girl with a dream.

"I can do this," she whispered to herself. "I can." Then she went back out to her spa where her skillful hands, her blissful creams, her soothing spa atmosphere worked as they always did to boost her confidence.

She was checking e-mail later that day when she saw one from her accountant, Nigel, and her heart skipped. She'd come to rely on him, even if Dennis the menace had been the one to introduce them. Nigel was smart, hardworking and averse to risk, which was probably a good balance for her enthusiasm.

Mercedes,
We've got a tentative financing commitment from your banker. When we met to go over the business plan, I wasn't sure you flirting with him was a smart business move. Guess I was wrong. He says you can go ahead and start scouting locations.

She decided to overlook Nigel's comments on how she did business. She did not flirt. Not exactly. It was more like she let men feel good about themselves in her presence. And what was wrong with that? Besides, they were getting the financing.

Oh, yes! Her heart pounded now. She was close to her dream. So close.

Her eyes danced to the next line of the e-mail and then widened in horror.

I've sent the package on to Dennis McClary, your lawyer. He'll need to be involved with any contracts. Give me a call when you've got some time and we'll get together and go over the details of the financing.

Best, Nigel

She'd been standing, bending over her computer screen, but now she plopped into her chair as though somebody had kicked the legs out from under her, which, in a way, they had. How could Nigel do that? How could he think for one second that Dennis was her lawyer?

Her eyes closed. Of course he would think Dennis was her lawyer. Dennis had introduced them. To Nigel, who'd been married long enough to produce two school-aged children, it was probably much more likely that Dennis would send a client than a lover.

It wasn't something she and her accountant had ever discussed. Theirs was purely a business relationship. Just the kind he assumed she had with Dennis.

"Ay, carajo!" Mercedes muttered, her eyes already fixed on that wretched business card tucked into her mirror.

Sino, her *abuela* would say. Twice in one day, she'd been pushed toward Dennis. Fate.

She tapped a perfectly manicured nail on her desk. Where she came from, a woman didn't mess with *sino*.

A shudder rippled over her skin. Dennis. Once she'd thought he was her *destino*. Now, she just needed a lawyer she could trust.

2

DENNIS MCCLARY BARELY LIFTED his gaze from the deposition he was reading when his direct line rang. It was his mother. He knew her ring.

"McClary," he said curtly into the phone, trying to telegraph he was a) busy, b) disinclined to hear how lovely he and Theresa Lampcott had looked together at the benefit on Saturday night and c) that he didn't care how much she wanted grandchildren, he wasn't ready to settle down.

"Did I catch you at a bad time?"

He damn near dropped the phone. The sultry voice on the other end was not his mother's. This voice had the same effect on him as the soulful wail of a sax in a smoky bar when the jazz quartet had finished their set pieces and were jamming for their own pleasure and that of the few diehards still hanging around.

"Mercedes," he said. "It's good to hear your voice." Too good. Way, way too good.

"It's been a while."

Eight weeks, three days and—he glanced at his watch, two hours or so. "Has it?"

The silence between them crackled. It had been

physical and intense between them from the moment they met. They'd burned up the sheets, the town, the very air between them. Then they'd, quite spectacularly, blown up. Always, even at the end, it had been fiery.

He wanted to jump in and ask her how she was, where she was, and did she want him to come right over? But he was a lawyer, disciplined, he hoped, restrained. She'd called him. It was up to her to state her business—preferably before he made a fool of himself.

"This is awkward," she said at last, sounding extremely reluctant.

"Do you need help?" His heart bumped. When a person informed a lawyer they needed help, it usually meant somebody was in an unpleasant situation. "Are you in trouble?"

"No." She released a breath and he knew in that instant how much she didn't want to be making this call. "Didn't you get the package from Nigel?"

"Maybe. If it wasn't urgent, I haven't got to it yet." He calmed down, knowing she wasn't calling him from jail.

"Oh. I see." How that voice could get to him, to that deep part he didn't spend a lot of time exposing. He could picture her lips forming the words. He could actually see those full, red lips, moist and utterly kissable, mouth the words. They'd purse when she said, "oh," as though she were puckering up. "You are still practicing corporate law?"

"I haven't changed professions in the last eight weeks," he snapped. Then screwed up his face at his error. Now she knew he was intensely aware of the last time they'd seen each other.

However, if she realized he was still a head case over her, she gave no sign of it; merely said, "I won't keep you now. You're the only decent lawyer I know. I want to hire you."

"I'm the only *decent* lawyer you know or the only lawyer?"

She was startled into a tiny chuckle. "Both."

"After the way things ended between us, I thought you'd go to the yellow pages before you'd come to me." Screw it. Why should he act polite? She'd thrown him over, and it still hurt.

"I thought of it," she admitted. "Nigel says I can start scouting locations for the new spa now. He wants you to look over the business plan and the financing papers and prepare an offer to lease in case I find anything."

For his ex-girlfriend to be asking this of him seemed a little like knocking a guy's teeth down his throat and then asking to borrow his toothbrush. "You want me to do up a contract as a personal favor?" he asked, keeping his tone perfectly even.

"No, of course not. I'm hiring you."

Surprise had him lifting his brows.

"Let's not get too far ahead of ourselves. I have no idea if I have time. My workload is crazy, I'm going to trial next week and—"

"And you're not sure you want to see me again."

"Oh, I know I want to see you again."

And this time, he thought, this time, the relationship would be on his terms. He had let her take him over, mind and body, for three amazing months. Then she'd tossed him out of her life for the most unfathomable reasons.

She'd left him ragged and scarred. Very much a burn victim of a passion that flared too hot. Yet he'd known they would see each other again. It was inevitable, living and working in San Francisco, that their paths would cross. And when they did, he'd be ready.

He hadn't imagined that she'd call him out of the blue, however, and try to hire him.

No. The last time he'd seen her, she'd been wearing a black and red silk robe, her eyes flashing fire and she'd yelled at him in a combination of English and Spanish, then thrown a heavy saucepan at him, followed by a lit pillar candle.

No, he hadn't expected a business call from her. Forgetting about the deposition for the moment, he reached for the day's mail. There was a package from the accountant, all right. He slit the envelope and pulled out a sheaf of papers. Flipped through them quickly.

"How fast do you want to move on this stuff?" he asked as he skimmed.

"Pretty fast."

"Come in for a meeting. I'm not sure of my schedule—"

"I could e-mail you—"

"No. I'll transfer you to my secretary. She keeps my appointment book. Sort out a time that works and we'll meet in my office." Where he was in control. He'd make sure there were no heavy objects suitable for throwing at him.

He thought she'd refuse. Almost hoped she would. He felt her struggle, then she snapped, "Fine."

He smiled, enjoying the small feeling of triumph.

"I'll look forward to seeing you again," he said, and then transferred the call before she could respond.

Mercedes Estevez. He leaned his head back in his chair and allowed that sultry voice to play through his mind again. He opened a desk drawer and, almost furtively, pulled out the photograph he'd shoved to the back of the drawer after they had broken up. He'd taken it when they'd been out on his boat, and her thick, dark hair was dancing in the breeze. Those dark, dark eyes were laughing, her lips curved, that amazing body barely contained within the halter top and shorts she wore. Everything about her pose invited him. She wasn't posed provocatively, but he had only to glance at that picture and feel the searing attraction—and to remember how, right after he'd clicked the photo, he'd taken them to a sheltered bay where they'd gone at each other wildly.

He shook his head against a surge of unwilling lust. "Unfinished business, Mercedes. You and I have some unfinished business."

The biggest piece of unfinished business was the way they'd parted. She was a good enough shot that his hair had been singed when that burning candle hit him. It should have blown out long before impact. All he knew was, he'd had to take scissors to a singed chunk of hair above his right ear. He shook his head. Passion, he'd discovered, had its dark side.

Well, she'd been right about one of the things she'd yelled at him that morning. Tempestuous Mercedes Estevez would never be an asset as a politician's wife.

MERCEDES DRESSED with more than her usual care. She needed an outfit that would at once proclaim, "Business woman not to be messed with," and perhaps most important, "No way you are ever getting me out of these clothes again."

These were somewhat contradictory messages to expect out of one outfit, so it was no wonder that an hour before she was due at the law offices of Dunford, Ross and McKay she was still in her underwear, an impressive mountain of rejected clothes on her bed and her closet emptied.

That's when she realized she had completely lost her perspective. She didn't put herself through this for anybody. What was she thinking?

She pulled a favorite red dress from near the top of the pile and held it against her. Red was a power color, good. Also the color of passion. Not so good.

She had a boho skirt in blues that went with a great peasant blouse. Another favorite outfit. Also new in the last nine weeks. She dragged the two pieces out and considered them. Blue was cool. Professional. But the bohemian style was too college girl/starlet perhaps. Definitely not a power look.

No, she decided, knowing it was time to make a decision and stick with it. The red.

When she was in the dress, she had another qualm. It fit where it touched, and the neckline did more than hint at her cleavage. Oh, too bad. She slipped gold hoops into her ears and left her neck bare. Too much jewelry tended to detract from a professional image.

Slipping on heels and giving her lips a last swipe with

clear gloss, she grabbed the slim briefcase she rarely used, and headed out the door.

She'd built an extra ten minutes into her timetable in case of unforeseen holdups and found she needed every one of them. She'd bought her town house in the Mission District with her grandmother's help not long after she'd opened Indulge. Her grandmother didn't believe in renting when a person could own, and so she'd bought a town house in a neighborhood coming up but still full of life. In a couple of blocks she could stop at a *panadería* and eat tiny cakes almost as good as her *abuela* made, shop at colorful boutiques or simply sit at an outdoor restaurant and feel the sun on her face as she ate good food and watched the world go by.

Today, traffic was heavy and parking would be a nightmare, so she took the Muni, arriving on the fifteenth-floor offices of the law firm only two minutes late.

And if J. Dennis wanted to bill her for the two minutes of his wasted time, he was welcome.

"Good afternoon," said the polished receptionist with a cool smile. Mercedes was so glad she'd never come to his office when they were going out. To the receptionist she was only a client.

"Hi. I have an appointment with Dennis McClary. Mercedes Estevez."

"Yes, of course." The woman checked her computer. "I'll let his assistant know you're here. Please have a seat."

Mercedes settled into one of the leather club chairs that belonged in some men's club smoking lounge. In spite of herself, she glanced around with curiosity. There was a mahogany table in front of them, with a fan of current affairs and business magazines. To her left was a built-in bookcase housing, naturally, leather-bound law books. An orchid bloomed—polite and unobtrusive—in a blue pot.

Mercedes wanted to run.

A slim young woman in a navy suit and sensible pumps emerged and she was treated to another professional greeting. "I'm Camilla Leeson," she said. "Won't you come this way?"

The woman couldn't be more than thirty, yet her skin looked tired and dehydrated. To Mercedes, every woman she met was like an artist's canvas. Some were finished to perfection—like most of her clients. Some were half-done, and she itched to complete the picture. Some, like this one, needed serious work on the canvas before any paint should be attempted.

What Ms. Leeson needed, and badly, was an exfoliating treatment, a deep moisturizing facial, a lesson in makeup and a new haircut.

If they had a chance to chat, she'd mention her business, maybe find a way to slip one of her complimentary intro cards to the woman. It was tragic to watch an attractive young woman make so little of her potential. However, there was no time for chatting. After a walk through sinfully thick carpet to an open doorway, they were there.

Ms. Leeson knocked on the open door—heavy mahogany to match the rest of the decor—and ushered Mercedes inside.

She plastered a cool, remote smile on her face and stepped into an office that had young-lawyer-on-the-rise stamped all over it. At that moment the young lawyer did rise, from behind an eight-foot mahogany desk, and stepped toward them.

Their gazes met.

She'd expected this first meeting to be awkward, to feel a little flustered. She'd been prepared for that.

What she hadn't expected was to be body-slammed by lust so strong and fierce she took a single, stumbling step backward before she regained control. In that second she'd recalled the way he looked at her when they were making love, the way his body felt intimately connected to hers.

Of all the cards in that wretched boot, why the hell did she have to pick his?

Destino? Fate couldn't be this sexy.

3

DENNIS'S EYES WIDENED the tiniest fraction, a movement only Mercedes could see, and she knew he was as shocked at the strong current zapping between them as she. This was a big mistake, she realized. She wanted to turn and walk out of there while she still could, but he'd rounded the desk, with his hand extended, lawyer to client.

"It's nice to see you again."

As she took his hand, he leaned in and kissed her cheek, as though they were casual acquaintances. She wouldn't pull back, that would make an issue of it, so she allowed him to brush her cheek with his lips, hating the way every cell in her body perked to attention as he neared.

He looked the same. Brown hair trimmed close. She'd liked it when it got long enough to start curling, which was exactly when he cut it. His gray-green eyes looked as serious as ever. Was she the only one who saw the molten lava beneath the cool surface? He wasn't supertall, maybe five-eleven, but he was solid. His jaw was square, his cheeks on the lean side. His nose just beaky enough to save it from being pretty.

He smelled the same. So very familiar. So very dangerous.

He was bad for her. Terrible in every respect but one. Bloody hormones. Why couldn't they show some judgment?

There was a round conference table in the corner of the office with four chairs. He ushered her toward it, pulling out a chair for her as though he were a maître d'. He sat facing her. He had a file folder, no doubt stuff from her finance guy, a fresh legal pad in front of him and a fancy-looking pen. Probably a family heirloom, handed down through generations of Mc-Clary lawyers, judges, senators and governors. Ms. Leeson took a third chair, Mercedes was happy to note, glad this wasn't going to be a meeting for two.

"So," he said calmly. "I've reviewed the documents Nigel sent over. Your expansion plans are impressive." He glanced up. "It's pretty aggressive."

"I know." Then, she decided, since she was paying him for his expertise, she might as well avail herself of some. "Too aggressive?"

He pondered her question, glancing through the sheaf of papers in front of him, which gave her a chance to sit back and study him. What was there about this one, of all the men she'd met, that was so special?

He was good-looking in a crisp, groomed, Ivy League way that wasn't her usual style. He'd never been pierced or tattooed, she knew from close inspection. She knew he'd never grown his hair long, because she'd asked him. Never rebelled in any way from the path he'd been born to travel. The only remotely wild thing he'd ever done, she imagined, was to hook up with her.

His body was good. But she'd known better. Well, the

guy worked sixty hours a week, no way he could spend hours a day working out, but for a desk jockey he was pretty fit.

He was steady, predictable, the kind of man who knew at thirty where he'd be at sixty. She was driven and easily bored. She wasn't sure where she'd be tomorrow. How could two people so opposite in every way have connected so deeply?

"No. It's not too aggressive for you. You know what you want, the financing seems solid, and you've got a track record."

He stared down at his notes for a moment, a tiny crease appearing between his brows.

"Well?" she asked, impatient as always. "What are you thinking now?"

"I'm thinking Indulge is you. It's your baby, your vision, and your personality is stamped all over it. The single spa is doing really well. But will a chain of spas do as well? There's a lot of competition out there."

"My concept is unique. My products are special. I've got an agent scouting out locations." The excitement was in her voice and in her body. She wouldn't let fear in. She didn't believe in being negative.

"Look, I can't tell you that this will pay off, because I don't know." He motioned to the other woman at the table. "Camilla will do some additional research if you'd like."

"Wow. I thought lawyers mostly sued people and wrote wills."

He sent her a "No, you didn't" glance, but, presumably for Ms. Leeson's benefit, he played along with her. "Our firm does a lot of corporate work. We like to make sure your interests are protected from the very beginning. You can get a contract written or reviewed anywhere. Nigel and I work a lot together, protecting clients."

"From themselves?"

He grinned at her, and damn but she wished he wouldn't. Too sexy. Too warm. Too intimate. "Sometimes."

If anybody had been protecting her from herself, she wouldn't be sitting here right now. Since she was, she'd better focus on her business and give her libido the afternoon off.

"I know I'm ready to start expanding," she said, her confidence strong, heating her from within. She smiled. "That's why I'm the entrepreneur and you're the lawyer."

He nodded, giving her a half grin. "We always were opposites." There was a moment, one of those emotion-charged moments, like before a first kiss, when the air around them tingled with everything they were feeling and everything they weren't saying. She gazed into his eyes and recalled how they looked when they darkened with passion, the intense expression on his face when he entered her body, the way she'd run her fingers all through his hair and it would never muss.

It had been more than two months since she'd seen him, yet she knew the taste of his mouth on hers, the feel of his body when it was tight against hers.

He was feeling the same things, she knew it. "I miss you," his eyes told her. She glanced away before she could send back the same message.

Then Camilla Leeson interrupted the weird moment as though she hadn't felt the tension in the air. "I've got a few questions and some suggestions of areas you might like me to research."

So finally Mercedes was able to concentrate on what she was paying these guys for. They talked for half an hour, and at the end of it she'd agreed to let Camilla work with the scouting agent on selecting potential locations, and Dennis was going to do a lot of boring-sounding stuff that would protect her assets and her ass as she proceeded with the expansion.

When they were done, they all rose and headed toward the door. "I'll call you," he said, and her heart did a very stupid, very irritating lurch before she realized he meant he'd call about work.

More than ever she wished she'd told her finance guy to tell Dennis he'd made a mistake. She could have pulled any lawyer's name out of the yellow pages.

Then why hadn't she?

DENNIS WATCHED Mercedes's back all the way down the hall. She was easy to spot. The lady in red. In an office full of suits that ran the spectrum from charcoal to navy, she'd have stood out even without the lush beauty and the sexuality she exuded like some exotic perfume. He watched the sway of her hips and the strut of her long legs in flame-colored high heels until she turned the corner and was lost to view, at which point he shook his head, hopefully hard enough to slide his brain back into place. It wasn't that he was lusting after her; he simply couldn't keep his eyes off her.

He'd been intensely aware of her the entire meeting, even when he appeared to be studying the financial pro-

jections. He'd noticed when she'd shifted in her chair.
When she'd uncrossed her legs and changed position,
he'd almost stumbled over a word. He'd felt her heat,
caught the elusive scent of herbs and flowers that he
knew she used in her beauty products. She'd rubbed so
much of it into so many skins that it seemed to have
become a part of her.

The red dress was perfectly proper business attire,
so why had he wanted to tear it off her? Preferably
with his teeth?

Truth was, Mercedes Estevez didn't do prim. She'd
pinned her hair neatly back, but it only made him long
to pull out the pins and watch the cascade of black silk
tumble down her back.

No, he decided, confirming what he'd known since he
first heard her voice on the other end of the phone; he
wasn't nearly done with her yet. She could have contacted
any one of a dozen lawyers who would do as good a job
as he could. Hell, if she'd asked him for a referral he'd have
given one. But she hadn't. She'd asked him to help her
expand her business—asked him to help her fulfill her
dream.

She'd reopened the lines of communication between
them and he chose to think that there was more than
business on her mind. He was almost certain he'd seen
the shock of lust slam into her exactly as it had slammed
into him. You didn't walk away from a connection that
deep, that visceral.

While he was helping her fulfill her business dreams,
he had to find a way to fulfill his very carnal dreams of
Mercedes or he was likely to go out of his mind.

He worked the rest of the afternoon, the certain knowledge that he'd see her again humming under the surface. He could write up a generic offer to lease and punch in details when she'd firmed up her next location, but instead he preferred to take a more active role in helping her. Her ambition had always impressed and amazed him. The flip side of her ambition was her impatience—her Achilles' heel. She could all too easily rush into an expansion and he didn't want to see her make a mistake. No. Camilla would do her research, and he'd do a little research on his own, because whatever had happened between him and Mercedes, he wanted her to succeed. He'd do some fact finding and call her in a few days. Waiting all that time would about kill her.

Grinning to himself, he thought he'd enjoy making her wait almost as much as he'd enjoy seeing her again.

Of course, the tough part was knowing that he'd be keeping himself waiting, as well.

Still, last time they'd been all fire and greed and that hadn't worked out so well. Maybe patience was something they both needed to practice if they had any hope at all of making this crazy thing work between them…because he'd taken one look at her in his office and known he had to have her again.

This time though, it would be on his terms.

At six he packed up and left, walking past Camilla, hard at work. "Night, Camilla, don't work too late."

His first-year associate glanced up at him vaguely as though she'd forgotten where she was. As a researcher she was formidable, and if he didn't know how fiercely determined she was to get ahead he would feel guilty that she stayed after him so many nights. She didn't seem to have much of a social life—a definite asset in a legal firm. He knew her as a tireless worker with a keen mind and he had no doubt she'd end up a partner at a very young age.

"Good night, Dennis. See you in the morning."

CAMILLA LEESON RUBBED her eyes before turning back to her computer screen. There went Dennis. Not so many years older than she, not so very much more successful, and yet they were light-years apart.

He'd be off somewhere tonight, no doubt. Some intimate dinner with a woman who was as confident and exciting as he was. A woman like Mercedes Estevez, she thought. In the office with the two of them, she'd been afraid she'd get a third-degree burn if she accidentally got between them. The first time they'd ever met and they were practically melting each other's clothes off their bodies with the power of their mutual attraction.

What would it be like to be a woman with that style, that glamour, that…oh, hell, that sexuality, Camilla wondered. She had never felt quite so dowdy and drab. She'd bought her suit at Lohmann's for a great price, even though it was a size eight and she wore a six. Until Mercedes had walked in today, she'd thought she looked as good as a professional woman ought to look. Then the woman in the red dress and the attitude had entered the law office and she'd noticed every eye on her. Not only the men's either. She had a presence, a style and yet she managed to look businesslike. Camilla glanced down at herself. Her suit was basic navy and her blouse was a sensible white. Her pumps were neither high heeled nor flat, but somewhere in between.

Oh, God. She didn't look like a successful business woman. She looked like a flight attendant.

Where did Mercedes Estevez shop, she wondered, recalling how that vivid red dress and the woman in it seemed made for each other.

Every once in a while Camilla would decide she needed some new clothes and she'd determine to buy something a little more trendy than the classics she bought because she was never sure whether something was good trendy or bad trendy, the height of fashion or a season too late. So, she would end up with more of the same. Very respectable, very dull clothes so classic they'd never go out of style because they'd never really been in.

Oh, well. It didn't matter whether men stared at her so hard they didn't even hear a person talking to them, like Dennis had done with Mercedes. She didn't have time for a man. All she ever did was work. And for the next year or so, that's all she'd be doing.

But, she reminded herself, it was going to be worth it. One day her name would be on the firm's letterhead, too. Then she could worry about her clothes. Ha, by then she'd be pulling in a big enough salary that she could hire a personal shopper.

And with that pleasant thought, she turned back to her computer screen and lost herself in work.

EVEN THOUGH HE'D LEFT before Camilla, it was still close to six-thirty when he strolled out of the building into a mellow September evening. He was thinking maybe he'd go for a run before the sun went down when everything inside him went still.

There was Mercedes standing, watching him. She'd changed her clothes since he'd seen her earlier. Now she wore a pair of faded jeans and a crisp white cotton shirt—sleeveless so her toned arms were bare. She had sandals on her feet and her toes peeked out, polished a pinky-brown color he liked.

"I was waiting for you," she said, leaning against a lamp as though she couldn't be bothered to move.

He knew her, though, enough to tell that she was keyed up. There was a tenseness to her body that belied the casual attitude.

"Hope I didn't keep you waiting."

She shrugged. "Not too long."

"You could have called."

Her hair swung as she shook her head—as dark and shiny as a shampoo commercial. He was glad she'd let it down. "I like to see people when I'm talking to them about something important."

Another suit on his way out of the building stopped dead when he saw Mercedes. She barely noticed. It happened to her all the time. She had an aura of glamour about her that made people stop and look twice, wondering if she was one of the Latino starlets, a Salma or Penelope taking a break from Hollywood.

After one more longing stare at Mercedes, the guy shuffled on his way. Her complete unconcern at the male attention amused him. "How many men tried to make time with you while you were standing there?"

She shrugged. It was no big deal. "A few."

"Let's go somewhere and get a drink," he said, immediately deciding he didn't need a run after all.

"I want to talk to you."

"My brilliant legal mind deduced that fact. And I want a drink. Come or don't come."

With an exaggerated huff, she fell into step with him as he headed to the closest place he could think of, an outdoor patio in an upscale boutique hotel not far from his office.

They sat in metal chairs with a small round table between them. Leafy trees overhead threw patterns on the table, the tiled floor and Mercedes's skin. He studied her. How had she grown more beautiful than his memory had painted her?

He felt the energy radiating off her as if she was sitting but yearned to be up and doing. He was never sure how she managed to provide a soothing spa atmosphere when she was so restless. She didn't fidget or tap, she remained outwardly still, but the energy was there—he felt it—more potent for having no outlet.

"Well?" he asked.

"I need an update."

He shook his head at her, squelching the impulse to laugh. "It's been less than five hours since our meeting. What could I possibly have that's new? Besides, I'm not sure how I feel about you showing up outside my office for updates," he said.

"I'm impatient."

"I remember."

For a second their shared past shimmered between them and then she shook her head as though she could make the past disappear. "I'm worried that my plan is insane. You made me doubt myself. I hate that."

Reminding himself of his promise earlier, that this time he'd be the one calling the shots, he rose, slipped off his jacket and hung it on his chair back. Then he loosened his tie, pulled the thing all the way off and stuck it in his jacket pocket before sitting down again. "I'm on my own time now, honey. Let's sit, have a drink, catch up." He rolled up his sleeves and was feeling a lot more comfortable.

"But—"

"You want to talk business outside office hours? Then we do it my way."

She was still glaring at him when the waitress came by for their order.

"A margarita, please," Mercedes said.

"Beer for me." He specified the kind and then he was alone with Mercedes, watching in some amusement as she struggled with herself. Would she tell him to go to hell, as she no doubt wanted to, or would she play nice?

She decided to play nice. "How are you?" she asked, shifting forward, a tiny smile tilting the corners of her mouth.

"I'm fine. Busy, you know, but good. You?"

"Also fine. The spa's very busy. And—"

"How's your family?" He wasn't going to let her drag him right back into talking about her business.

"My *abuela* still runs the family farm. She's got help, of course, but she drives us all crazy. She won't take it easy at all." She shrugged, in a what-can-you-do way and he thought she had nabbed a lot of her own personality from her *abuela*. Interesting that when he'd asked about her family, her grandmother—the matriarch of the family—was the first one she mentioned. Not her mother, her deadbeat father or her sibs. One day, he thought, she'd take over as the matriarch. He wondered if that made him nervous, and found that all he felt was pride.

"Abuela's so proud that I'm expanding my spa concept."

Her eyes sparkled with excitement the way, he imagined, they'd look when she talked about her child if she ever had one.

"You are a lot like her," he said. He'd only met her grandmother a couple of times. She was a force to be reckoned with. He'd liked her enormously.

Mercedes sent him a sunbeam of a smile that almost took his breath away. "That's the nicest thing you've ever said to me."

"Well, it's true. You come from a family of strong women. You are one."

Her smile dimmed. "Abuela's the only one in my family who doesn't think I'm out of my mind to expand so soon. I guess that's why I need to know what you really think."

It was his turn to feel flattered. Outside of bed, they hadn't ever really spent much time in each other's worlds. He was gratified that she cared about his opinion.

"Isn't Nigel giving you good advice? His is worth a hell of a lot more than mine when it comes to financial considerations."

"He's a good accountant," she agreed.

"Right. Also smart and cautious." In addition, the man

was incredibly homely and happily married. He couldn't believe he'd once been that jealous over this woman.

"You're right. He's given me very good advice. Stops me being too impulsive…at least he tries."

"Poor bastard."

She glanced up, momentarily startled, then laughed. "So, I'm impulsive. Okay, now we've caught up. What do you honestly think?"

"I've got Camilla doing some research on locations, rents and so on. I know it's not strictly what you hired us for. I don't want you making a mistake."

She shook her head. "A researcher. Wow."

"She's a first-year associate, basically an overworked drone paying her dues until she makes partner."

"She could be a lot brighter."

He nearly choked on his beer. "Do you have any idea what you're talking about? Camilla was top of her class at UCLA School of Law. She is one of the brightest women I know, and the hardest working."

Her laugh was sudden and warm, as unbidden and welcome as sunshine after a shower. "I didn't mean bright as in smart, I meant she could be a lot brighter in appearance."

He tried to bring up a mental picture of Camilla and all he got was an image of a conservatively dressed woman. "What's wrong with her appearance?"

"Dull complexion, tragic makeup, dead hair." She sent him a mischievous grin. "Nothing a day at the spa and some strategic shopping won't fix."

He shook his head slowly. "I don't think she's the spa type."

"*Quérido,* everybody is the spa type. Some just don't know it yet."

"I'll tell you one thing for damn sure. I'm not the spa type."

She sipped her drink slowly, then licked salt from her lips with a deliberate gesture that made him half-crazy with a sudden urge to kiss her. She caught every glistening salt crystal with the tip of her pink tongue. He couldn't take his eyes off her freshly moistened lips and, damn it all, she knew it.

"Honey, I could do things to you on a spa bed that would have you begging for more."

"Isn't that illegal?" he managed to croak.

She leaned back and regarded him from under her lashes. "I was talking about my Indulge Him facial, foot and hand treatment. Three hours inside my spa and you'll be booking your next appointment when you leave."

The notion of having her hands on him for three hours was right up there with his ripest fantasies. Not for a facial, though. "I don't know."

"When you help me get my second location up and running, I'll throw the package in as a tip," she said, rising to leave.

His chair thwacked the tile floor as he lurched to his feet after her. So much for suave and cool, he thought, as he threw a bill onto the table, grabbed his coat and scrambled after her like a new puppy.

"Wait!" he said when he caught up with her on Front Street. She turned, sexy and long and infinitely desirable. "What's your rush?"

"I have to be somewhere."

"Hot date?"

Her glance was cool and snooty; however, she didn't do cool and snooty well. When she firmed her full lips they turned pouty and when she narrowed her eyes she merely looked sultry. Underneath he could see the heat churning within, part annoyance and part unwilling attraction. He recognized the combination since he was a victim of the same mix of emotions. Finally she said, "You're my lawyer, not my lover."

He strode up to her, getting right up close and personal until her head tilted so she could glare up at him.

"Maybe I'm not your lover now," he agreed, "but we both know it's going to happen soon."

"In which daydream?"

"You came to me," he reminded her.

"For business reasons," she said, taking a step back.

He followed so he was once again well inside her personal space.

Her eyes crackled with emotions. Irritation, attraction, no less powerful for being unwilling, and wariness.

Smart woman. She should be wary.

"I don't think we finished catching up on our personal news," he said, and before she could argue, back away or even guess his intention, he did what he'd been wanting to do since he heard her voice on the phone.

He pulled her against him and brought his mouth down on hers.

4

BY THE TIME SHE'D TAKEN IN the astonishing fact that her very expensive lawyer was kissing her, desire had snuck under the lid she'd slammed over her libido.

Her lips remembered him; her body remembered him. He kissed with purpose and finesse, easing her into heat even as he prevented her retreat with a hand at her back.

For one blind second she pulled back from him, panicked at the way he could make her feel and how devastating the consequences would be if she ever again allowed herself to fall under his spell. Then the inevitable tide rolled through her, hot and liquid, and with a tiny moan she fell into the kiss.

She heard the thud as his briefcase hit the pavement, and then they were wound around each other, all lips and tongues and heat.

They might have stayed that way for days, but a soft wolf whistle brought her back to her surroundings with a start.

"You're one lucky dog," said a good-looking black guy sauntering past.

Dennis never took his eyes off her face. "I know," he said.

She put a hand to her hair, horrified, embarrassed and ridiculously turned on. "I can't believe you…I…we…"

"Come back to my place," he said, his voice not entirely steady. She'd bet any money this wasn't what he'd intended. He'd wanted to throw her off balance, which he had, but he'd ended up teetering on the edge of reason himself. She was almost certain he hadn't planned on that.

She shook her head. "No. This is crazy. I have to be somewhere."

"This isn't going away, you know. When you're ready to face it, call me."

Sudden fury overwhelmed her, it erupted fast and seemingly out of nowhere, like a volcano. "Face what? We were great together. The sex was fantastic, but the relationship wasn't going anywhere. Ever."

"That's not what— I didn't…"

She stepped backward, away from the heat of his body and the attraction compelling her to him. "We burned up the sheets, babe, and that was fun. Remember I've got a spa empire to build and you've got your family's traditions to live up to."

"Mercedes, wait."

She was already walking away, trying very hard to believe what she'd told him.

He grasped her arm, forcing her to turn and face him. The pavement was rough under her feet, the air fresh with the smell of the bay. "You were so busy throwing things at my head that night, that I never completely got what I'd done wrong."

"Which is why you never bothered to phone and find out?" she asked him sweetly.

"Hey, when a guy's cutting off his singed hair and wondering what hit him, both physically and emotionally, it takes some time."

She drew in a deep breath and made herself relax. "Look, we could stand here and bicker forever. I'm going to cut you some slack. Sure, we still have some animal attraction."

He snorted.

"Okay, a lot of animal attraction going on. I hired you to be my lawyer." She wrinkled her brow. "Anyhow, isn't it unethical for you to sleep with your clients?"

"Not unless you've committed a crime," he told her loftily. "And you must be crazy if you think we're not going to end up in bed again if we start spending a lot of time together. This," he said touching her shoulder with one finger and then gesturing to his chest, "this thing between us is…unbelievable."

He had a point. One kiss and she'd wavered for a second when he asked her to go back to his place. A man who could give her the explosive passion that had consumed them for months…he was tough to walk away from. Even now she was tingling in some very inappropriate places while she turned him down. She knew herself well enough to realize she wasn't going to be able to keep away from him even though she knew he was bad for her. Bad, bad, bad.

Unless she had a foolproof strategy. And the easiest way to get him to back off was both obvious and hurtful. "How long did we go out?" she asked.

"Three months," he said.

"Three months, twelve weeks, approximately a

season." She watched his eyes, hazel eyes that changed color depending on the weather, what he wore and his mood. Chameleon eyes she called them. "And what did we do during that time?"

He appeared confused and, in true lawyer fashion, seemed to be searching for the hidden meaning, or the trick in her question. "Do?" he finally repeated. "We did what couples usually do. We went out."

"Mostly, we stayed in," she reminded him.

His eyes went hot at once, darkening so she knew he was imagining them in bed together, exactly as she'd meant him to. "Yeah," he said, reaching forward as though he couldn't help himself, taking strands of silky hair and running them through his fingers. "We stayed in a lot."

It was a stupid little gesture, yet the way he looked at her, and the tiny brush of his finger, wound with her hair, against her cheek was as potent as the deepest kiss. How did he do this to her?

How could she let him?

Right, she couldn't. She tossed her hair over her shoulder, effectively dislodging his hold. "Exactly. In three months I never met any of your friends, we barely ever went out the door."

"What are you talking about? We ate out a lot."

"Ha, sex fuel."

He grinned. "Call it what you want. You weren't complaining."

"I'm still not complaining. We never met each other's friends, apart from my *abuela,* we never met the families. I think we both knew it was a short-term thing, so we never bothered to act like a couple."

"What?" he sounded truly astonished. "That's crazy. If you wanted to meet my friends, why didn't you ever say anything?"

Because she'd wanted him all to herself.

"I will never forget how guilty you looked when your mother and father came into the restaurant that night." The bitter memory remained clear.

"They caught me with my hand up your skirt. You'd have been embarrassed, too."

"They didn't know anything about me." The woman he'd been making love with an hour earlier.

"Well, so—"

"Did they?"

"No."

He gazed up now, a belligerent expression on his face. "I hadn't wanted to make a big deal of it, that's all. So what? We had dinner with my parents, which apparently is what you wanted all along and never bothered to tell me."

There was a moment of intense silence between them. She heard traffic, a woman's laughter from somewhere, the noise of a busy kitchen gearing up for the dinner trade.

"I wanted you to be proud of me," she said at last, "proud to be with me. Proud to introduce me to your family."

"I was proud," he insisted.

She skewered him with a glance. "Bullshit. You bolted your food, you were so anxious to get out of there, and when your mother asked all those pointed questions you made me sound like a casual friend, some girl you'd known for a couple of days."

"Look, you don't know what my family is like. All I wanted was for us to have some privacy, some space. I never meant to hurt you."

"Well, you did hurt me." Strange, she hadn't acknowledged until now that it had hurt. At the time, she'd felt royally pissed that he acted so casual, not seeing below the surface to where her deeper feelings hid.

"And instead of calmly telling me how you felt, you threw half your apartment at my head and then threw me out."

"I was angry."

"You were a natural disaster. Hurricane Mercedes."

"And you never called or tried to see me again."

"You threatened to cut off all my best parts if I tried."

"That's not what stopped you."

He sighed, his gaze steady on hers once more. "No."

"You didn't call because you were scared of your family's disapproval."

"No," he said. "That's not it."

"What, then?"

"I'm not sure I can explain." He shoved his hands in his pockets and rocked back on his heels. He was really thinking about this, she decided, and she sensed he was trying to be honest. "It suddenly felt like everything was crazy. You were acting crazy, work was nuts, and I wasn't sure what I wanted, I guess."

"So you dumped me. Just like that. One dinner with your folks and I'm history."

"Oh, come on. Who was the one setting whose hair on fire and throwing the hissy fit of the century? I'd say you were the one doing the dumping. I kept waiting for you to call."

"I was waiting for you."

His eyes were steady on hers. Gray green in this light, intent and focused. "Maybe we both needed some space."

She wanted to throw herself into his arms and leap right back into the amazing passion and excitement they'd experienced together for three glorious months. She was smarter now, more careful with her ego. And her heart.

"Maybe we still need that space."

"What do you want, Mercedes?" He was touching her hair again, as though he couldn't help himself, and she let him, enjoying the soothing feel of his hand, the tiny erotic thrill as her own hair caressed her shoulders, neck and cheek.

For whatever reasons, whether *destino* or pure, Sisters of the Booty Call coincidence, she and Dennis had entered each other's orbits again. Maybe it was time to see if there was anything but hot sex between them. So she told him the truth.

"I want to be written up in *Barron's* as the next Estée Lauder or Helena Rubenstein. I want my products to be available all over the country and for women from Wichita to Waikiki to be able to sample a little bit of Indulge." Then she took another breath and hoped what she was about to say was also the truth. "I don't have time for you complicating my life right now. Maybe when things calm down…"

He took an involuntary step back, as though she'd slapped him, hard. "You don't mean that."

"You don't have time for me, either. What about your

political career? I read in the paper that you're being groomed to be the next McClary in public office."

"I haven't decided—"

She held up a hand. "All I know is that great sex is all we had, and when I accidentally ended up meeting your parents I felt—I can't even explain it. I felt like I wasn't welcome in that part of your life."

"Is it at all possible that you overreacted maybe a little bit?"

"I don't know. Maybe."

He blew out a breath and said, "I'm really sorry if I hurt you."

"I know. I'm sorry I lost my temper."

"Well," he said smiling down at her in that bone-melting way he had, "that wasn't so tough, was it? We both apologized for acting like fools. Maybe there's hope that—"

"I don't think so. I'm busy now, busier than ever. I haven't got time for a full-time man."

"Why don't you let me finish," he said. "I have an idea."

"If it involves taking my clothes off, I'm not interested."

"Liar," he said mildly, though with a gleam of humor. "Here's my idea. I'll call you up. We'll go for a date."

"A date."

"Yes. An antiquated term, I know. Two people meet and go for dinner or a movie. In this case it's a charity thing." He shot her a considering gaze from under his brows. "My family will be there. You can meet my sister. Get to know my parents better. And don't tell me you don't have time. There will be influential people there, who would be good for you to know. Money people, powerful people. Part of your business is getting out there. You'll never be written up in *Barron's* without investors taking an interest in your business. These are the kind of people who can help."

"Oh." Suddenly, she wished she'd kept her mouth shut. Did she really want to face all of that on her first actual date with this guy?

She knew he was doing his best to give them another try. Dating. Slow and easy. What a concept.

"Do you remember where we met?" she asked him.

"Sure. Salsa night at that Latino club near the Wharf. You had a white dress on. I took one look at you shaking it out there on the floor and I damn near swallowed my tongue."

"You remember what happened next?"

"I walked up to you and asked you to dance. You said yes." His voice lowered a little, and he touched her back, where his hand had first rested. "You were hot. There was a glow of perspiration on your neck and the swell where your breasts came out of the top of the dress. I touched you and you felt like sex."

"And then?"

"Then I bought you a drink. A margarita."

"What did you have?"

His grin was quick and wolfish. "A tequila shot. With lime. And the salt I licked off your skin."

He was getting turned on thinking about it, as was she, but there was a point to this trip down memory lane. She watched him lick his lips as though he were tasting the salt of her skin, and a quiver ran through her. What was she doing, playing with fire like this? She could almost feel the shock of his warm, wet tongue on her upper breast, the way he'd seduced her with his eyes, the way she'd known they'd be lovers before she even knew his name.

"Then what happened?"

"We danced some more. And then we went back to your place."

"And then?"

"Don't tell me you don't remember the next part?" His voice was rough, the way it got when he was aroused.

"We were naked and going at it the second we got to my place." She tried to glare at him, but it was impossible. "I'd never done anything like that before. It wasn't until I was trying to call out your name that I realized I didn't even know what it was."

He chuckled. "I remember that. I'm naked, you're naked, we're going at it like wildcats and you stopped and said, 'Perhaps we should introduce ourselves.'" He threw back his head and laughed. "I think you even shook my hand."

"I was taught good manners," she said, trying not to smile.

"I really think we should go back to my place right now and get to know each other again."

"You are missing my point. Look at the way we met, how it all started. It was always about the sex. From the beginning. We did it all wrong. Started in the wrong place."

"I know. Can't you see that's what I'm trying to fix? We'll date. Like normal, totally boring adults. We'll go to a stuffy charity gala, and I'll escort you home afterward and maybe ask for a second date if we have a good time."

She bit her lip, tempted though uncertain. "I don't know. We started at the wrong place," she insisted.

"We ate dessert before dinner. So what? We'll do it over. This time we'll go slowly, start where you're supposed to." He touched her cheek. "Maybe we'll get dessert twice."

"When is this charity thing?"

"I forget. Truth is I wasn't even planning to go. This way, I can introduce you to everybody at once. Very time efficient."

Oh, joy.

"I'll call you with the date."

"Okay." She half hoped she'd find she was already busy that day.

5

WHAT WAS HE DOING? Dennis asked himself that about seven times a day. He hated those stiff, boring society things. He hated the very idea of subjecting Mercedes to one of them, yet listening to her, he'd suddenly seen her point. He wasn't ashamed of her. He was crazy about her; all the same he hadn't been thrilled at the idea of subjecting her to his family. She was vital, alive, sexy and exciting. His family—apart from himself, he hoped—wasn't.

Coming, as he did, from old money, old family, old established traditions, had plenty of negatives as far as he could see. The basic one being some dusty notion that he was somehow predestined for politics. Even though his family had provided California with one governor and half a dozen judges, he didn't have to follow that route.

Fortunately, he'd fallen in love with the law from the moment he began to study it. Maybe that part of his heritage was in his blood. Nonetheless, he didn't feel any inclination at present to follow any of his illustrious and not-so-illustrious forebears into politics.

In spite of the odd scandal, the few rotten apples that gave the whole bushel a bad name, he respected the law and he believed in it. He also believed in democracy and its responsibilities and duties. He'd never missed voting. Not once. Whether it was a municipal vote, a local referendum or a presidential election, he treated them all equally seriously. However, that didn't mean he wanted to play in that arena.

His mother and father hadn't quite accepted that fact.

To them, his showing up at this shindig would probably be taken as a sign that he was starting to move into the social circles he would need to cultivate if he decided to seek elective office.

So, he had his family issues to face.

A prickling sensation traveled the back of his neck when he recalled how she'd described his behavior when they'd run into his folks at some restaurant. He had been uncomfortable. Horribly so. Afterward he'd been troubled and confused by his own behavior, but astute enough to realize that something had been going on. Something he still needed to sort out.

So, he would take Mercedes to the stuffy banquet. He would introduce her to everybody he could think of, let them see him with a woman who was important to him, then he'd escort her home, with all due politeness.

A kiss on the cheek, maybe. That should convince her he wasn't always a sex maniac where she was concerned.

Well, he was a sex maniac where she was concerned, but for one evening he could control himself.

At least he could try.

BE CAREFUL WHAT YOU WISH FOR. That old saw had never felt so true as it did when Dennis called. Mercedes had been waiting for his call—obsessively checking her voice and e-mail and racing to check her Call Display every time the phone rang. When he finally did phone, two days after he'd told her about the date, she was there, so she was able to decide whether she preferred to get the news on voice mail, giving her time to make up an excuse, or whether she wanted to actually talk to him.

Surprise spiked in her gut when she grabbed the phone up the second she recognized who was calling.

"Hello?"

"Mercedes, it's Dennis."

"Hi." Oh, breathless anyone? Feeling foolish to have butterflies cartwheeling around her belly?

"You still up for this date thing?"

Abruptly she stopped feeling nervous when she realized that he was as much of a wreck over this thing as she.

"I don't know. Tell me about it."

"Well…" She could tell he was picking up the invitation, imagined the look of it, all expensive cream vellum and fancy I'm-richer-than-you-are script.

"The Friends of the San Francisco Ballet Society requests the pleasure of your company blah, blah, blah, Saturday the tenth for dinner to be followed by dancing. Wow. Those wild and crazy dogs. Or do you think it's the ballet company dancing?"

She chuckled softly. "I have no idea. I love the ballet, though."

"Me, too. I'd rather buy season's tickets."

"You don't want to go."

"Yes, I do." He lied so badly for a lawyer she couldn't believe it. "If you go, I want to go."

She checked her calendar. "Well, as it turns out, I'm free Saturday."

"Okay, great. I'll pick you up at seven."

"All right." She wondered if, now that he had her committed for an actual date, he'd try to fit something into the intervening days, but, to her surprise, he didn't. "Okay, then."

"Okay."

"You haven't moved or anything?"

"No. I live at the same address."

"Great. Well, I'll see you next week."

"I'm looking forward to it."

She wandered into her next treatment wondering what to wear. She figured she had two options: dress for Dennis's mother and her crowd, the ones who would be judging her or dress for herself. For most of her life she'd dressed to please herself. For the first time in years she considered dressing for someone else.

When Camilla Leeson left a message, asking Mercedes to come to a meeting in Dennis's office Wednesday, she saw through the ruse right away. She'd been hot and twitchy ever since their passionate kiss had heated up the sidewalks, so it didn't surprise her at all to find that Dennis had found an excuse to meet with her before their formal date on the weekend.

She'd imagined Dennis would engage her in a meeting of style and no substance for half an hour or so, after which he'd casually suggest an after-work drink or dinner to continue discussing the spa expansion, whereupon he'd use his considerable charm, and her own weakness, to entice her back to his place. Her place.

A parked car. A treehouse. Any one of a thousand places where two very aroused people could be alone for some hot and heavy personal business.

Wednesday at 3:00 p.m. she was met once more at the reception desk of Dunford, Ross and McKay by Camilla Leeson and ushered into Dennis's office.

"Dennis is on a conference call in another lawyer's office. He asked me to apologize and tell you he'll be about five or ten minutes. Can I get you something while you're waiting? Coffee? Tea? Mineral water?"

"I'd love some mineral water. Thanks. You should have some, too."

Camilla Leeson blinked her pale lashes and said, "Pardon?"

Mercedes looked at the overworked young woman, and her fingers itched to get that face into her treatment room, hooked up with a decent hairdresser, and then into the hands of a personal shopper. She was wearing a suit almost identical to the one she'd worn last time Mercedes had been here. Her makeup was limited to eyeliner applied with a wobbly hand and the remains of a pale lipstick, most of which had worn off.

"Sorry," she said, "professional hazard. I noticed that your skin is dehydrated. You need to drink a lot of water in the day, especially when you work in an air-conditioned office. If you're drinking coffee, cut it way down."

The woman's eyes widened. They were a pretty blue, and a little makeup would make the world of difference by drawing attention to them. "It's diet cola, not coffee. I'm addicted to the stuff. It's what got me through law school and gets me through the long hours here." Her hand crept to her cheek and Mercedes silently added a manicurist to the list of professionals this woman needed. "You can tell all that by looking at me?"

"Yep."

Since she didn't seem offended by Mercedes's frankness, maybe she was ready for some more nudging in the right direction.

"You want some more free advice?"

Camille appeared skeptical. "In my business, that's an oxymoron."

Mercedes grinned. "In mine I guess it's marketing."

"Okay. Hit me."

"You need to exfoliate. Three times a week. I'd also recommend you get more sleep, make sure your day cream has an SPF of at least thirty, and—" She stopped when she saw the expression on Camilla's face. "You do wear day cream?"

"Look, I've been working pretty much every day, evening and weekend since I started law school," Camilla said. "No. Before that. I put myself through school, so I always had jobs as well as a heavy load." She ran a hand through her unfashionable hair. It wanted to be blond. It was dying to be blond. And it was almost there. "I use soap, water and whatever's on sale at the drugstore."

Struggling not to shudder Mercedes took one of her introductory cards out of her bag and handed it to Camilla. "This is a coupon for a free facial and consultation about skin care." She smiled. "No obligation, I promise, and I can have you in and out in an hour."

"An hour? Really."

"I promise. Hey, I'm busy, too. I know the value of

time when you work long hours." She hesitated, not wanting to be rude. "I also know the value of good skin care. I can help you look beautiful now and keep you looking young much longer than soap and water and drugstore bargains will."

Camilla studied the card carefully. "Are you open after work?"

"After work, lunch hours, weekends. I'm sure we can find a time that works for you."

"I'll think about it. Thanks." And she left the room.

"You give away facials?" Dennis asked, coming into the room as Camilla left. He waited until the associate was gone, but only barely.

"She could be really gorgeous with some help. Did you see that bone structure? And those blue eyes? No. Of course you didn't. The eyeliner kills them. I bet that once she discovers how much she likes looking and feeling better, she'll become a regular customer."

He glanced at the empty doorway Camilla had passed through. Shrugged. "If you say so. Sorry I'm a couple of minutes late. Can I get you something?"

"No, thanks. Camilla's getting me some water."

"Excellent. I asked her to sit in. She's been doing some research for you."

When Camilla returned with a tray, containing a glass of mineral water, Mercedes noticed that she'd poured herself a glass, too. Progress.

Mercedes raised her brows at Dennis and received a gaze warm enough to scorch her skin, but other than that, she could be any client. Her first guess, that he'd invited her here to hit on her turned out to be false. So did her second assumption, that he'd invented some fluffy reason for the meeting, when Nigel Brewster, her accountant, walked in.

"Hi, Nigel," she said.

"Good to see you, Mercedes."

"I asked Nigel to come, too," Dennis said. "Makes it easier if we're all on the same team. We'll call it the expansion team. I've prepared an offer to lease, which can be tweaked for a specific location. Nigel is concerned about capital outlay, and I'm concerned about making sure your butt is covered legally. Camilla's been doing some research I think you'll find interesting."

"Wow," she said, feeling as if she'd suddenly made it in the world as she gazed at her two lawyers and her accountant. "I have an expansion team."

6

DENNIS FELT AS foolish as a kid on prom night, riding up to his date's house in a limo. He hated acting pretentious, and to him riding around in limos was right up there. Still, he'd decided to prove two things to Mercedes tonight.

One. He was capable of acting like a gentleman and had some social skills.

Two. Their relationship wasn't all about sex. Nevertheless he was determined to act as though it were the last thing on his mind.

The limo pulled up outside her town house. Her grandmother had lent her the money for the down payment when she'd first started out, five years ago. Neighborhood prices had skyrocketed since. He thought, as he had many times before, that her sultry good looks hid a very sharp brain. Smart girl. He adjusted the unfamiliar bow tie on his tux and knocked on her door.

It opened and there she was. She was a beautiful woman who always dressed stylishly. Tonight it was obvious she'd put extra effort into their date, as he had.

Her dress was coffee-colored silk that fell in drapes

to her ankles. The scoop of the neckline revealed the swell of her breasts. Amber beads dangled from her ears and encircled her neck.

Her hair was up, with a few curls framing her face, and whatever she'd done with her makeup had her glowing.

"You look...amazing," he said.

"Thanks." She reached behind her for a silk shawl thing that matched the dress and a tiny purse with gold and silver beads all over it.

She stepped out and looked up the street before her gaze came to rest on the sleek black boat of a car. She glanced at him, her eyes so dark they appeared black, and then she chuckled. "A limo?"

"Don't make me feel stupider than I already do," he grumbled.

"It's very glam," she said, then turned completely, lifting her hands to fix his bow tie which had somehow gotten crooked. Again. Probably when he'd swallowed his tongue when he first saw her tonight.

The movement was intimate, almost wifely.

"Thanks," he said.

The driver, a big man in a uniform, held the back door open, and Mercedes slid in. He got in behind her and decided one of the benefits of a limo was that he had his hands and attention free. He reached for her hand and dropped a kiss on her wrist. Damn if he didn't feel her pulse jump against his lips.

That same elusive scent that was part of her teased his senses. Her skin was satin beneath his lips, and that ridiculous kiss on the wrist had him feeling as aroused as though she'd stripped.

She raised her startled eyes to his. He could tell from their clouded expression that she was feeling it, too. One move, one tiny move and they'd be all over each other. The heat swirled around them. Her pulse was quick and shallow beneath his fingers and her eyes widened. Her lips parted and he felt his body hardening for her.

All he had to do was kiss her and they'd both be lost. They'd arrive at the banquet disheveled and very, very satisfied, or more likely they'd never make it at all.

Fine by him, he thought, as he moved slowly closer to those moist, inviting lips. He hesitated, drawing out the moment of anticipation.

Then, like a bucket of ice water thrown over him, he remembered that humping in the limo two seconds after they'd left her place was not so fine for his plan.

So he closed his eyes, then giving her wrist a quick squeeze, placed her hand back in her lap.

"How was work today?" he asked, grasping for a subject that was neutral and wouldn't make him think about how much he wanted this woman.

"Work?" she asked, moving away from him as though she needed the space. "Um. Work was fine."

"Busy?"

"Busy." She shook her head. "Saturdays always are. I'm going to have to hire another aesthetician for weekends. If I can find a good one."

"That's great."

"Yes. It is." Her lips curved. "I had a new client today."

"Did you?" He couldn't stop watching her mouth. He was obsessed with it. As they drove through the streets, light played across her face, highlighting her moist, glistening lips.

"Mmm-hmm. Camilla Leeson."

Surprise had his gaze jerking to her eyes. They were looking pretty smug. "Really? Camilla?"

"Yep. She booked for a one-hour facial, and I could tell she hated to leave. She's already booked for a more extensive treatment next week. When I'm finished with her, she's going to look better, feel better and carry herself with a lot more confidence."

"Just don't mess with her legal brain."

"Don't be stupid. I'm merely repackaging her legal brain. Believe me, you'll like the results. More important, she'll like the results."

She looked so pleased with herself, as though she'd really done Camilla a service. "You really get off on this stuff, don't you?"

"Of course I do. I believe every woman deserves to be pampered and that every woman has her own beauty. Sometimes they need to find it. Sometimes they simply need to believe in it."

"So, did you take your own advice today? Were you pampered?"

She laughed. "Hardly. We were packed. Lunch was an apple and a Snickers bar. My feet are killing me." She shrugged. "How about you? Did you work today?"

She'd obviously remembered that he often went into the office on a Saturday. Usually sandwiched between a morning quickie and a late-afternoon orgy. "For a few hours."

She nodded and he didn't feel inclined to pursue the

subject of his boring afternoon at work. He fiddled with his bow tie again.

"Are your family really going to be here tonight?"

"My mom and dad, maybe my sister. You'll also meet a few of my friends. Some business acquaintances."

"So, getting loaded, dragging you under a banquet table and doing you would be inappropriate?"

He swallowed so hard the guy up front must have heard him. "No," he said, when he got his voice back. "I think that would be very, very appropriate."

An impish grin lit her face. "I'll think about it." The car slowed and she said, "Oh, it looks like we're here."

And so they were. The limo pulled smoothly in front of the red-awninged doorway of the St. Francis Hotel in Union Square and the driver hopped out to open Mercedes's door for her. She eased out, stopping to rearrange the folds of her dress, and when she was done, he took her hand.

"It's upstairs. Thirty-second floor," he informed her, as they ascended.

The gala was held in two glass-walled restaurants and, even though he'd eaten here before, he'd never seen it decorated quite so…lavishly. White net stuff and pink silk, which he supposed were representative of tutus, decorated everything.

Oh, boy.

He passed his invitation to the greeter and then they were inside. Yep, it was as bad as he'd expected. All the who's who of San Francisco society. A buzz of conversation, crowded tables, a string quartet playing middle-of-the-road jazz. And beckoning to him, like a director pulling her star onto the stage, was his mother.

"It's showtime," he whispered to Mercedes. She glanced up, saw his mother, and he felt her body tighten. Not in a good way, either. Firmly holding her hand, he led her forward.

"Mother," he said when he reached her side, kissing the perfumed cheek she offered.

"Hello, darling. A lot of people are here who want to meet you," she said significantly. People, in his mother's terms could only mean the power players who could help him in his political career, should he decide on one.

"You remember Mercedes?" He put an arm around his date.

"Oh. My. Yes. I didn't expect—" He rarely saw his mother stumble socially, and she caught herself now. She extended her hand. "How nice to see you."

Mercedes shook her hand briefly. There wasn't exactly a lot of chemistry between these two.

"Dad," he said, giving his dad a hearty handshake.

"Hello, son. Is Theresa with you?"

"No. Remember Mercedes Estevez?"

"Hello, Mr. McClary," she said, giving him her hand. Dad was having none of that, and gave her a smacker on the cheek. Mercedes didn't seem at all bothered. He had a feeling she'd perfected her distancing skills from overfriendly men of all ages about the time she bought her first training bra.

"Well, isn't this nice," his mother said. "A real family party. We're table seventeen. I think you'll know almost everyone."

"Wonderful. Mother, I'm going to take Mercedes and mingle. We'll see you for dinner."

"Do that, dear. The senator is in the far corner beside the ice sculpture. Why don't you go and say hello?"

He sent her a cheery wave and bundled Mercedes out of there. Waiters were wandering around with champagne and hors d'oeuvres. He nabbed a couple of glasses and passed one to Mercedes.

It was the usual crush of the monied, the who's who, the climbers, the wannabes, some media, most of the San Francisco Ballet company and the genuine ballet lovers.

Usually he hated these things. With Mercedes by his side, he found himself actually having fun. She was so alive. And interested in everyone, moving from a discussion with a ballerina about skin care, to chatting with the senator's wife about Mexican culture. She charmed without effort and, though she never pushed, she ended up being asked for her card by a lot of the women present.

He decided, watching her laugh at a mild joke made by the senator, that she treated everyone the same. Rich or poor, important or not, it didn't matter to her. She liked people. And they, in turn, warmed to her.

When any of the men eyed her like the hors d'oeuvres, he'd wrap an arm around her shoulder or kiss her cheek in blatant and Neanderthal warning.

Dinner was less fun. Theresa, a woman he often squired to these things if neither of them had a date, was seated beside his mother. His mom had made no secret of the fact that she thought Theresa would be an ideal match for him. Seeing them together was like seeing a mother-daughter pair. He liked Theresa fine, had known her most of his life, and they had a lot of friends in common, but he didn't want to marry a younger version of his mother. And he wasn't remotely attracted to her.

His mom didn't give up easily. So, between his mother dropping comments into the conversation that would only be understood by people who shared the same background, and him trying to explain every one of them to Mercedes, and Mercedes laughing and flirting with a male principal dancer at their table—weren't those guys supposed to be gay?—and his father dropping hints as subtle as scud missiles about his political future into the mix, Dennis was getting a headache.

The auction was better as it kept conversation at the tables to a minimum. He hadn't known Mercedes had donated until he heard them announce the prize, a his-and-hers day at the spa, which generated some spirited bidding. When the final price was announced, Mercedes clapped, her cheeks pink with pleasure. "I can't believe it went for so much money."

"The money's for charity, dear. You won't get it yourself," his mother pointed out.

"Mercedes knows that, Mom. She's excited that she was able to generate so much money for the ballet."

"On behalf of the ballet, allow me to thank you," said the dancer on the other side of his date in a Russian accent. While Dennis watched, the Russian kissed Mercedes right on the mouth. His date didn't seem to mind a bit.

"I'm happy that so many people here wanted to come to my spa," she said. "It's a good thing when you can support a worthy cause and promote your business at the same time."

"You know, honey," he said later, when they finally got back into the limo for the return trip, "you are the one who should go into politics. I never knew you were so good with people."

"It's because we rarely saw anyone but each other when we were together," she reminded him.

"I was a lot less jealous then."

She laughed. "And that's something I learned tonight about you."

"Was I too possessive?"

"Ya think? If we were dogs you'd have peed on me."

"I don't think dogs pee on their mates. It's usually trees and things, to mark their territory."

She waved away such unnecessary details. "The point is, you were overbearing, possessive and—"

"I couldn't help it. It was that dress. The way other guys were checking you out. Every man in there wanted to go home with you tonight."

"And yet I'm here," she said, her eyes glittering. "With you."

Their eyes met and held. The flicker of heat that he'd felt between them all night flamed. He wanted her so badly it hurt.

But he'd made a promise to himself tonight, and he wasn't about to break it. She thought he was more interested in having sex with her than in simply being with her. He had to prove to her that wasn't true.

Well, it wasn't completely true. The absolute truth was he wanted both.

It all seemed quite complicated, and he hoped very much that she would soon understand that he liked her and not only the incredible sexual chemistry between them.

Preferably before his balls turned blue and fell off.

Suddenly it seemed like a stupid idea to have ordered the limo. If he was driving, he'd have something to do. An activity that would keep him too occupied to reach for her. Especially as she seemed to be expecting him to lunge for her. Her eyes were dark and expectant, her lips glossy and slightly parted, so he saw the white gleam of her teeth.

He dragged up some small talk and ended up telling her a totally boring story about some old rich guy who'd come in to have a new will written. By the time he realized his story had no point, she was looking distinctly amused as though she knew exactly what his problem was.

"I'll have to remember to update my will," she said after he petered out.

Fortunately, before he had to drag something even more inane out of his repertoire of boring work anecdotes, the limo pulled to a halt.

The driver came around to the curbside door and opened it. Mercedes exited and Dennis followed. "Wait for me," he said in a low voice to the driver, who nodded, giving him a glance of surprise and what looked like derision.

Dennis walked her the short distance to her door. She took her key out of that minuscule excuse for a purse and turned to him, with raised brows. "Would you like to come in?"

"Yes. But I'm not going to."

She blinked, slowly, as though she couldn't believe what he was saying. Truth was he could barely believe it himself. He took her face in his hands and gazed down into her beautiful big brown eyes. "I promised you a certain kind of date, and I try to be a man of my word. As much as I am going insane with the need to make love to you, I'm going to wait."

"How long?" she asked in a whisper.

"Until I know you're as ready for this as I am." Then he kissed her, slow and sweet. Teasing her a little. So she sighed when he turned and walked away.

The driver was holding open his door, and he was about to climb in when she said, "Dennis?"

The tone of her voice alone had the painful ache in his groin hitching up another notch. It was as though her voice could reach out across the pavement and caress him with wispy, intimate fingers.

He turned and a soundless moan emerged from somewhere deep in his chest.

She was looking at him from under her lashes, her eyes gleaming provocatively, her chin dipped down a little. It was a classic sex kitten pose. And her hands were busy at her dress. She'd undone the front of her bodice, so the laciest excuse for a black bra showcased her glorious breasts. They stood out, rising and falling with her rapid breathing.

"I'm ready now," she said softly.

7

FOR A SECOND he couldn't seem to coordinate his body, brain or mouth. He was stalled there, one foot in the limo, the other on the pavement, staring like a fool.

She cocked a hip and sent him a teasing look. "Well?"

And suddenly all his synapses snapped into place. "I won't be needing you anymore tonight," he told the driver.

"No, sir," the guy said in a much huskier tone than he'd used before.

"And quit staring at my date."

"Yes, sir."

Dennis, finally coordinating his brain to send the correct messages to his legs, sprinted to Mercedes. "Are you crazy?" he asked, his throat so hoarse with wanting her he could barely get the words out. "Anybody could see you. You're practically exposing your—"

And before he got to the end of the sentence, she snapped the opening of her bra and the lacy cups fell away like a curtain opening on the big show.

Light from a nearby streetlamp acted like a spotlight, showcasing her body, drenching her in gold.

Words failed him as her naked breasts were revealed. She cocked a hand on her hip, draped from belly to toe, her torso naked, looking for all the world like an ancient Greek statue come to life. Venus de Milo, with arms.

He didn't bother searching for words. It was hopeless. He bent, put an arm under her knees, another around her shoulders and hoisted her in his arms. She started to laugh softly, but he shut her up with his mouth on hers. She threw her arms around his neck, kissing him, wriggling against him so his lust spurred, fast and furious.

Fortunately, she'd already unlocked the door. He got them both through it, then he kicked the door behind him, hearing the solid thunk as he shut the world out.

They were in the foyer of her town house. He felt his desire spike. They'd never yet walked through this door without falling into each other's arms. But he'd been without her so long, had started this evening with strict instructions to himself not to do this. So to find himself really here, about to make love to the woman he'd lusted after since the second he met her, was almost too much. He felt shaky with need, his skin overheated, his muscles tense.

"You can let me go now," she said against his mouth.

"Never," he muttered back, kissing her again, so their mouths were fused as he started up the stairs to the main living area, where her bedroom lay. Halfway up the stairs, she let out a little squeak. "My dress."

The comment didn't even register on his lust-soaked brain, until he stepped onto the slippery fabric and lost his footing. They tumbled. Thankfully the stairs were thickly carpeted and softened the impact. Instead of rising again, he kissed the mouth laughing up at him, feasted on her mouth, filling his hands with her breasts.

She was making little panting noises, eager cries that told him she was as overwhelmed by desire as he.

Her bedroom might as well have been on the moon. They were not going to make it.

He ran his hands feverishly over her. Her skin was warm and so silky and smelled exactly as he remembered it: like all the flowers and spices of her grandmother's garden in late summer and of her own spicy scent. It was in her hair, on her skin, in the air around them. Drawing him, bewitching him.

She was tugging at his jacket. With a few fevered pulls he'd dragged his arms out of the thing and tossed it over the banister. They tugged and pulled, clumsy with need and haste, until his torso was bare. He fumbled at his belt, so desperate to drive into her panting, writhing body, he could barely see straight.

Suddenly, he realized what he was about to do, and his hand froze. He was like an animal—no finesse, no thought for her, his manners gone.

Making himself slow down, he reached out to feather his fingertips over the sensitive tips of her breasts, the way she liked.

Her eyes were heavy, half-closed, her hair a wild, cocoa-colored curtain, her breasts hot to the touch. She moaned when he touched her, tossed her head back and forth like a fever victim. Then he felt her hands at his waistband. Her fingers were hot and shaky as she dealt with button and fly and then scooped his cock into her hand.

"Oh, baby," he mumbled, feeling as if his eyes might

roll back into his head and he'd pass out right there. "I don't think—"

"Now, *quérido,* now."

She wasn't caressing him, she was dragging him to her. Only now did he get it. She was as crazed as he.

"Okay, yes," he managed. He dug out his wallet, found the condom he always kept there, even though he hadn't needed one in the two months since he'd last been with Mercedes. In a second he had her dress down over her hips, and her lace panties down her legs. He looked up, and there she was, her knees falling open, and all her glory displayed. She was silky, wet, swollen. He reached a finger to touch her and found he was shaking. The minute he touched her she shuddered. "I wanted to take my time this first time," he said, knowing it was impossible.

"Later," she panted. "I need you now."

He might have been able to fight his own blind lust, however he couldn't hold out against hers. Rising, he threw himself over her, gripping the stair riser on which her head rested.

She reached for him once again, putting him where she needed him most. His eyes closed as he felt the soft, sweet spot trembling beneath him, felt the wet heat drawing him in. As he entered her, he knew that no woman had ever, or would ever, be able to make him feel this way. So hot, so needy but so absolutely right. He slid into paradise and felt her shudder as they connected.

Her knees came up, and she hooked her legs around his hips. She was hanging on to the banister rails, her hips pumping against him.

It couldn't last. All that heat and friction couldn't sustain itself without combusting. And in an embarrassingly short amount of time he did. His chest felt as if it would explode as he took her, feeling her quake and pant beneath him. Then that tell-tale cry that was probably his favorite sound in all the world began—the early warning that she was about to come.

His control had been shot to hell, anyway, and at that tiny cry, he lost it, going over the edge as her body shuddered and clenched, milking him of every drop.

For a long moment they stayed joined and panting, then he raised his head to look down at her, feeling mildly foolish. "You okay?"

"Apart from the rug burn on my ass." And she started to giggle, her dark eyes dancing, her hair splayed out over the stairs, the muscles in her belly quivering with laughter.

He joined in, couldn't help it. "So much for my elegant date, and treating you like a queen."

"I'm fine with the way you treated me," she informed him, rising upward to nip his jaw. "Now help me up."

MERCEDES, HAVING DECIDED in advance exactly how the evening would end, had stocked up on snacks and a few things she knew Dennis liked. Because, unless they'd both changed a lot in the past couple of months, they were going to need their strength.

She flicked on the gas fireplace in the living area, lit candles and said, "Help yourself to a beer or some wine in the fridge. I'll be right back." Only then did she bother to enter her bedroom to find something to wear. She slipped into the bathroom to clean up, then donned a black-and-red silk kimono she wore instead of a bathrobe. She brushed her hair and then, emerging, turned down the bed and smiled smugly at her Egyptian cotton sheets. You'll be getting a workout tonight, she promised them. Her body still throbbed, partly in satisfaction, partly in anticipation. They'd taken the edge off, still they weren't sprinters, she and Dennis. They were marathoners.

And they were just getting warmed up.

She returned to Dennis, who had pulled on his pants and his shirt, leaving it conveniently unbuttoned. In the formal wear, with his long bare feet poking out the bottom, his crisp shirt hanging loose and unbuttoned, he should have looked ridiculous, instead he looked mouthwateringly tasty. She licked her lips.

"I poured you some wine," he said, picking up two glasses and handing her one. They clinked glasses formally and sipped. "Mmm." He said. "That's a nice Bordeaux."

She stared down into the ruby-colored wine in her glass. "That's because you bought it and somehow I never got around to opening it." She shrugged, immediately wishing she hadn't mentioned the wine's origin. "What I know about wine, I learned from watching *Sideways*."

"And you call yourself a Californian."

"Half-Mexican," she reminded him. "Ask me about tequila."

He reached out and touched the skin of her wrist where it emerged from her silk robe. Flutters of sensation traveled up her arm like butterfly wings. His eyes were so serious; they always were.

"Would you like something to eat?" she asked, knowing they'd both picked at their food at the gala.

"No, thank you." His eyes traveled the length of her body, and beneath the silk of her robe, little sparks ignited up and down her skin.

She hit the play button on her CD player, not even sure what she'd last listened to, and was pleased to find it was Jennifer Peña, exactly right, another Mexican woman who knew about love and passion and wanting.

The fire flickered behind its screen, candlelight bathed the room in a sensuous glow that made the room both intimate and mysterious. The silk felt cool and luscious against her nipples, and she knew her skin was extrasensitive because of the way he was staring at her, arousing her.

"Would you like to sit down and talk?" she asked, hearing the husky tone in her own voice.

He appeared to consider the notion of a chitchat beside her fire.

"No," he said at last, regarding her steadily as though she were a witness he was waiting to crack under pressure on the stand. "I would like to make love to you again."

She bit back the smile. Though he might be serious, he was never dull. "All right," she said, wondering if he could hear her blood pound from where he was standing two feet away.

Probably.

He stepped closer and took her wine from her, placing both glasses on her coffee table. She bent for two of her beeswax pillar candles. She hated scented candles, hated the cloying artificial scents, instead she loved the honey and clover smell of beeswax, and the golden glow when it burned.

She carried the candles into the bedroom, and set one on each of her bedside tables, enjoying the pools of light. Apart from her brief time in the bathroom, she'd yet to turn on an electric light.

Dennis came up behind her and scooped his arms around her, cupping her breasts softly, then running his palms over the silky mounds, down her ribs and over her belly with slow, sensuous strokes. She leaned back against him with a sigh, relishing the lap of desire within her.

"This time," he promised, his words soft against her ear, "we take our time."

8

MERCEDES OPENED her eyes slowly, stretching luxuriously, a smile curving her lips. She heard soft breathing that wasn't her own, and as she turned her head, the memories of last night flowed over her.

Dennis was dead to the world, and she'd tired him out. Even so, her body tingled when she looked at him sleeping beside her, his face open and hers for the staring.

So she stared. Watched him sleep. Allowed herself to touch the cowlick that had sprung up in his dark hair. To notice the shadow of freckles under his morning stubble. His lips were finely molded and sensual even in sleep, his jaw more relaxed than usual, making him appear younger.

The shoulder rising over the sheet was strong with muscle, his arms defined and lightly furred below the elbow. One finger of his hand twitched in sleep, and she smiled, thinking of all that those hands had done to her and for her since she'd known him.

She retraced her gaze to his face and found his eyes half-open, watching her. In the morning light they were a cross between gray and green. He didn't speak, merely looked, and as she gazed back she wanted to laugh, cry and throw herself at him all at once.

The feeling frightened her so much that she closed her eyes against it, and against his too-intimate gaze. She kissed him. "Good morning, sexy," she said.

"Morning. What time is it?" He looked around for a clock.

"Why do you care? Do you have to be somewhere?"

"Squash game at ten." He shoved a hand in his hair and scratched his scalp. "No, wait, I canceled last night."

"You did?" She was strangely delighted. "When?"

"When we got back here last night. After the stairs. You were in the bathroom and I figured I was not going to be in any shape for the squash court today."

She laughed softly. "You were right. Don't worry, lover. I'll make sure you get your workout."

"Already did," he said sleepily. "I'm half dead."

"No, you're not," she told him, moving her naked body closer and rubbing up against him. She felt him spring to life immediately and laughed. "You are so easy."

He rolled her over and nipped at her breast, rubbing his stubbled chin over her sensitive skin so she was wriggling and laughing at the same time. "Stop it," she cried.

"I don't think so." And he didn't. He began kissing her breasts with slow care, taking his tongue to her nipples until she was lost.

Much later, after their shower, she prepared *huevos rancheros* while he brewed coffee. The morning was tranquil, domestic, and she thought how much she'd missed him, even though they'd only been together a short time before it all blew up.

He brushed behind her to fetch a spoon from the cutlery

drawer and ran his fingers down her back in passing, such a casual caress and yet it left shivers in its wake.

While she cooked the eggs, he passed her a mug of coffee with a dash of cream, no sugar. Exactly the way she liked it. He'd remembered.

They both ate with hearty appetites when the eggs were ready. She'd never been one to bother with diets and watching what she ate. Mercedes believed in eating well of good foods until you were satisfied, and plenty of fresh air and exercise. It was a philosophy she'd learned from the women in her family, and it had stood her well.

"Do you want to see a movie tonight?" he asked as though they were an established couple.

"I can't," she said.

He raised his head to stare at her. "You've got plans?"

She hesitated. Dennis was wrong for her in so many ways but one. She had to be careful about throwing herself back into the all-encompassing passion they'd known before.

"Yes," she said, refusing to elaborate.

He gazed at her for another moment. Since she obviously wasn't going to answer further, he leaned back in his chair, giving her that lawyer cross-examination expression that always pissed her off.

"You have a date?"

"That's none of your business."

His eyebrows rose. "We just made love about twelve times. I think that makes you dating another guy my business."

She thought about telling him that great sex did not make two people an instant couple but didn't have the energy for a stupid argument. "Well, it's not a date. It's business."

"Okay." He sipped his coffee, still watching her. "Look. I'm not a big one for 'having the talk' the second I sleep with a woman, still this doesn't feel new. It feels like we're picking up where we left off." He put the mug down, and it made a hollow sound as it hit the table. "Am I wrong?"

She hadn't wanted to have this talk so soon either, since she felt so mixed up. Her body was telling her one thing, her brain another. She had to try and sort it out.

If there was any hope for them, she needed to be honest. "Look. Here's what I think. We're…hot together. Maybe too hot. You know? I don't want to go through that again. It was too intense."

"What are you saying?"

"I'm saying I don't want to go there again."

"Come on," he said. Clearly thinking, as she was, that two people who clicked in bed the way they did, were going to go there again. "Let's be serious."

"No," she said, shaking her head so her still-damp hair swung. "Not serious. I made that mistake before with you."

"You're going to tell me this isn't serious? We couldn't get through that door downstairs before going at each other. In case you've forgotten, we couldn't make it up the damn stairs without tearing off our clothes and having sex so intense I've got carpet burn in some interesting places."

He did not have to remind her. Last night was branded on her memory like his touch was branded on her skin. "Oh, the sex is serious. Doesn't mean the relationship has to be."

"What the hell are you talking about?"

"I am talking about two people who share amazing sexual chemistry, of course. Long term—I don't know about that."

He looked totally frustrated and more than a little offended. "Do you want me or don't you?"

"Of course I want you." Even as she was thinking on the run, here, she kind of liked where it was going. "Whenever it works out. Look, I'm going to be away a lot, opening up the new spa, you've got a busy practice and the whole politician thing to do. When we're both around, we enjoy each other. Keep it simple. Have fun. When we're not available for each other, that's okay, too."

"You only want me for sex?" His voice rose on the last word as though he couldn't believe it.

"No. I want you for lots of things." She thought about it. "Yeah. Mostly sex."

"I am going to be your boy toy?"

She laughed, deep in her throat, delighted with the term and his annoyance. "That's exactly what I think you should be. My boy toy."

"What if I want more?" Dennis asked, wondering what he was doing, putting himself through this madness a second time. There she sat, across from him: her beautiful, big brown eyes half playful, half serious; her long, glossy still-damp hair pushed back over her shoulders; the tawny skin that was so exotic to him, as though she had a permanent tan.

He knew her body intimately, what made her sigh, what made her throw back her head and sob, the way that when he kissed the sole of her foot she giggled uncontrollably, and how, when he kissed the soft skin underneath her breasts, she broke out into goose bumps. He knew her. And yet she was a mystery.

Now her head tilted to the side, like a bird listening for movement. "Define *'more.'*"

"I don't know." He pushed away his plate, feeling out of his depth. "More. More than a fling."

"You want to be my boyfriend, dude?" she asked, with a deliberate teenage attitude.

"I want to be the man in your life. The only one," he as good as yelled. "That's what last night was supposed to be about."

"Oh, honey, no. Last night was a date. You wanted to see if I'd go through with it, show up at your snooty society do and make nice to your parents and their cronies."

"And you were great."

"Absolutely. And so were you. Neither of us choked when your mother thought Jennifer Lopez was the Grimwalds' latest cleaning lady."

"It's Juanita Lopez. Honest mistake."

She rubbed her red-tipped fingers into her hair so it cascaded over her shoulders. "I don't know. When I think of my spa, I see a thriving business that I've created. Your mom made me feel like I'm the manicure girl at the health club, you know?"

He gazed at her steadily. "She was trying to make it clear to you and me and the rest of the table that Theresa and I have a lot in common and you and I don't. It's her problem." He shifted forward a little. "Now I'm won- dering if she's the only one with a problem."

She rose, jerkily for such a graceful woman, so he knew he'd touched a chord. Even though he tensed his muscles and braced, she didn't throw anything.

Instead she stalked to the window and looked out, her back and shoulders rigid. Then she turned. "Maybe you're right," she said softly.

Progress, he thought to himself. Progress.

"I guess I've spent a lot of my life proving myself. I'm sick of it, you know? I'm smart, hardworking, talented."

"Mercedes, you are an amazing success. I'm proud of you."

She had the prettiest smile, and she gave it to him now. "Okay. I'm an amazing success. And people can only intimidate me if I let them."

"I wouldn't have put it in those Dr. Phil terms, but yeah."

"Okay."

"And guess what?" he said, knowing he had her.

"What?"

"I'm worth more, too. Forget this boy-toy shit. It's humiliating to me."

Her laugh rolled out, deep and rich as the best coffee. When she stopped, her eyes were still bright, her cheeks glowing, and he wanted nothing more than to take her back to bed.

"Here's the thing," she said. "You know I'm going out of town next week. I'm visiting a bunch of locations for future spas. If I find one, it's only going to get crazier in my life."

He didn't want her to go. He didn't want her off jaunting around all over California thinking of him as nothing more than a convenience. He didn't want to be the sexual equivalent of microwave popcorn. No, more than that, he didn't want her to leave so soon after they'd found each other again.

He didn't want to miss her the way he knew he would.

"What if I came with you?" The minute the words were out he wondered if he looked as startled as she did, staring at him with her mouth open and her eyes wide.

"Are you serious?"

Was he? He thought of a week without her and had his answer in a heartbeat. "Hell, yes, I'm serious. And as your lawyer I have certain skills that might come in handy."

Instantly she bristled. "I can do this myself."

"Of course you can. You should also be smart enough to use me."

"I just did."

He grinned, letting that obvious red flag go unchallenged. "You may not want to hear this. Listen anyway."

She looked wary, still she didn't try to stop him, so he continued. "Most of the guys who finance deals like this and who lease space are old school. They've got some preconceived notions. You go in alone. You're twenty-eight years old, way too gorgeous and sexy to possibly have a brain." He held his hand up as her mouth opened, stopping the tirade before it started. "And you're going to waste a bunch of time making them see how smart you are."

"They'll soon see I am."

"Obviously. Isn't it a waste of your time? You don't want to be selling them. You want them selling you."

"And that's where you come in?" she sounded pretty skeptical. "Because you've got cojones and you're all of thirty-two?"

"Because I'm a lawyer with an established, conservative firm. Plus, bringing me along makes you seem more important. Now these people see you have an acquisition team."

She glanced up at him under her lashes, which always meant she was up to something. "Maybe we should invite Nigel along, so they can see I've got a finance guy, too, as part of my acquisition team. He's another white guy for the team."

"Three's a crowd," he said.

She considered him.

"I can't believe you're offering to come with me. Are you sure?"

"Absolutely. I'll take my laptop and cell. A lot of my work I can do on the road. There's nothing that won't wait a week."

"It could be fun to have you with me."

"Camilla can stay on top of things at the office, and if there's an emergency I can fly back. I'll be your driver, your legal advisor, your sounding board and, most important, your sexual release."

For one more very long moment she stared at him, and he could practically see the desire warring with the doubt. Then, with the quickness with which she made all her decisions, she nodded. "You're on."

He hadn't realized how important it was that she say yes until he heard her enthusiastic agreement. Relief and an absurd excitement filled him. "Tell you what, why don't we leave Friday afternoon? Take the weekend for ourselves." There were places he wanted to show her, things he wanted to do to her and with her that took time. A weekend for themselves out of town. Why hadn't they ever done that when they were together? He was thrilled by the idea.

"Mmm. I'd love to. Friday after work and Saturday, though, are my busiest times at the spa. I could get away Sunday morning."

He narrowed his eyes like a gunfighter. "Saturday night. After you're done. We get a little pleasure in before you go to work."

"I'd like that. Thanks."

She looked at him, her eyes glossy with suppressed excitement. Her hair was drying with a funny kink in it that it got when she let it air dry. She wore her silk robe and nothing underneath. They'd made love so often in the past twelve hours that he should be drained dry, and yet he wanted her as eagerly as he had last night.

In that instant, like a blinding revelation, he knew he was in love with her.

Bang. Just like that. No fanfare. No big epiphany. He looked at her and knew.

And right then he knew he was going to wow her every second they were together. Maybe she wasn't any more ready to hear love words than he was to spout them; nonetheless, the truth was he was feeling them. Deep down in that place where he knew it was real.

He didn't know when or how it had happened, but he was falling in love with a maddening, independent woman who planned to be a cosmetics tycoon, not a politician's wife.

The question was, what was he going to do about it?

9

CAMILLA LEESON LEANED BACK in Dennis's chair for a moment and reminded herself that one day an office like this would be hers. And she'd be good to her associates the way Dennis was good to her.

He'd told her to use his office while he was away on his unexpected business trip. Well, he could call it business if he wanted to, but she'd booked the accommodations according to very strict criteria and it didn't seem like business was going to be a priority. She'd also noted that Dennis and his new client, Mercedes, only needed one room per stop.

Fast work, she thought, for two people who'd barely met. Of course, she'd noticed the instant attraction between them, but still, they'd gone from "How do you do?" to an intimate road trip staying at some mouthwateringly good hotels in less than three weeks. While she, Camilla, hadn't had a date in months.

So, there she was, sitting at Dennis's desk, working, but with a corner of her mind tracking the progress of the Mercedes-Dennis "business" trip like a mental GPS device when Jill called her.

Her old law school friend had ended up leaving

school early and now worked as a paralegal in her husband's firm. Jill and Wayne were her only married-couple friends and the only ones who seemed to care that she was single. Every once in a while, either strong friendship, an urge to interfere, boredom or maybe all three, would have Jill and Wayne trying to set her up with one of their unattached male friends.

After the minimum of pleasantries—they were both busy women—Jill said, "So, what are you up to for dinner tonight?"

Camilla's social calendar wasn't exactly jam-packed. She worked, she got home late, made herself some dinner or grabbed take-out, usually from her corner deli, tried to keep up with the news, maybe a little TV and went to bed. She managed movies with friends and on weekends sometimes went out. That was it.

She suspected Jill knew it.

"I don't think I—"

"Come for dinner with us. Wayne's old friend Jerry is in town. He's from Seattle but he's thinking of moving to San Francisco. He's very successful, and single." She pronounced the last word like a magician saying, Ta-da! "Wayne told him all about you and he wants to meet you."

Her first thought was that Wayne must have lied.

She was about to make up an excuse. That she had to work late was a good one. She didn't have time to go home and change and she wasn't even wearing her most flattering suit. Then she thought about Dennis and Mercedes. In three short weeks they'd gone from meeting each other to—Camilla didn't even want to follow her train of thought. She liked them both.

Thinking about them having wild sex seemed intrusive and inappropriate.

Maybe she and this Jerry would have chemistry from the first second they met...maybe. So she said yes before she could come up with a million reasons why this wasn't a great idea.

"Great," Jill said. "The four of us will have a ball. A double date." She giggled. "How fun."

Maybe it would be a lot of fun. Maybe she and Jerry would look at each other and there'd be that pow of chemistry. He'd be witty, charming, urbane. He'd see that beneath her admittedly drab exterior, was a loving woman waiting to be found. And her skin was certainly dewy since she'd experienced an Indulge facial and replaced the diet cola in her diet with water. She'd even splurged on the night and day moisturizers, the basic that Mercedes said were the foundations of ageless skin.

She touched her cheek. It was definitely soft. And, since she'd been using the cream, she felt prettier somehow, more womanly. Yes, maybe this Jerry would really see not just the efficient associate, but also the yearning woman. She pictured herself jetting off to Seattle for weekends snuggled together watching the rain, helping him find a place in San Francisco.

Camilla could even daydream and still get work accomplished. She printed the briefing notes she'd typed up. She needed a paperclip and was too lazy to walk back to her own desk for one. Where did Dennis keep his paperclips? She pulled open the top drawer and found pens, Post-it notes and a blank pad of paper.

Opened the side drawer. Ah, here they were, underneath a photograph. Dennis wasn't big on personal stuff cluttering his space, so she wasn't entirely surprised to see a framed picture in his drawer until she caught a glimpse of the woman in the photo.

She drew it out slowly, paperclips forgotten. Mercedes was in the picture. It had obviously been taken sometime in the summer. Camilla recognized Dennis's sailboat. She'd been on it herself once when Dennis had taken her and his secretary sailing as a thank-you for something or other. She, however, hadn't been wearing a halter top that showcased fabulous breasts, or shorts so skimpy the woman might as well not have bothered.

As she looked at that picture, Camilla realized she'd made a blunder. She'd assumed that Dennis and Mercedes had only met a couple of weeks ago here in the office. Clearly, that wasn't true.

The relationship she so envied wasn't an instantaneous attraction in the office leading within three weeks to a trip that would rival many honeymoons.

No, there was obviously something much more complicated going on. So much for simple and time efficient.

Sighing, she replaced the picture, remembering to get her paperclip first. Even when relationships seemed effortless, they weren't. Why couldn't love be easy?

She was still pondering that question halfway through her blind-date dinner. Jerry from Seattle turned out to be a lawyer. Of course. Jill and Wayne pretty much only knew other lawyers. So their conversation was predictably about cases, idiot judges, how many hours they billed, chances of partnership, etc.

Jerry was a perfectly nice guy. Still he wasn't particularly witty or charming or urbane, and he obviously wasn't big on seeing beneath the surface. She could tell right away that he wasn't taken by her any more than she was with him.

While she picked at her crab cakes it hit her she could be home right now, in her comfy clothes, curled on the couch with a bowl of ice cream and a good book. She glanced around the crowded restaurant and everybody seemed to be having so much fun. Couples in various stages of romance, from first love to old love, surrounded her. She was out on a date and she dreamed of sitting home eating ice cream?

Was there something wrong with her?

"Dessert?" Jill piped up when they'd finished their dinners.

Jerry jumped in before anyone else could say a word. "I don't think so. I've got to be up early. I should get going."

While Jill sent her a pitying look, Camilla was relieved to have the ordeal over with. Soon she'd be home and snug in her pajamas. Chocolate fudge ripple or praline ice cream? Which would it be?

THE HIGHWAY ROLLED AHEAD of them like a reel of film. Mercedes tilted her head back against the leather upholstery and stared up through her new oversize Chanel sunglasses, to the blue, blue sky above. The wind rushed at her, over her, around her, full of ocean breezes, dry grasses, definitely a hint of grape from the wine country.

Mercedes didn't know when she'd been this happy.

"I can't believe you arranged a convertible."

"I traded a buddy of mine cars for a week." Although Dennis sounded cool, like it was no big deal, she was still pleased he'd gone to so much trouble.

Ever since they'd crossed the Golden Gate Bridge after she'd left work—leaving Clementine, her senior aesthetician, to close up—she'd felt the thrill of adventure sparkle within her. Clem was the woman she would most likely promote to manage Indulge, San Francisco, once she was ready to open Indulge, somewhere else in California.

"Where are we going, anyway?"

"It's a surprise."

She turned to stare at his profile. His glasses were more functional than hers, wrapping around the sides of his head, preventing UV rays from mounting sneak sideways attacks. They also prevented her from reading his expression. "Surprise? We have to be in Calistoga tomorrow morning."

"And we will be." So calm. So in control. Such a lawyer.

"Okay." She shrugged. She was used to being in charge of everything from ordering new cotton swabs to pedicure chairs while living with the fact that she was risking everything to finance her dream spa company, so it seemed odd to be looked after, even for a day and a night. Odd but nice.

Knowing Dennis, they wouldn't be staying at the Motel 6.

They drove north on Highway 1, with enough traffic that she was glad she wasn't driving. "You know what's great about heavy traffic?"

"I can't think of one thing."

"More time to enjoy the scenery," she said, as they drove under ancient sequoia trees.

Even though she'd grown up in the area, she never got tired of watching the ocean. She imagined she never would. There wasn't a dollop of cloud or a wisp of fog out there today, only restless blue-gray water rolling in and back out.

After a while they turned inland, headed in the direction of the Sonoma Valley. She'd decided that would be her first stop, and Calistoga in particular because of its famed hot springs and mud baths. Maybe what that spa town really needed, was Indulge, Calistoga.

She had seven locations to visit. While each fit most or all of her criteria, she hoped she'd simply know the right one when she saw it. That's how it had happened with Indulge, San Francisco. That was the best way.

By early evening, they were in wine country. She loved the vineyards, the rows on rows of gnarly vines bursting with fruit. She could smell the fruit in the air.

They passed famous wineries and small boutique operations with silly or grand names. "I guess we're too late to stop in for a tasting," she said, glancing at her watch.

He turned to her and grinned. "We're not." Within minutes they were pulling into a gravel road with a carved wooden sign hanging over it that read, Château Chien. She glanced up again as they passed under the sign. "Château Chien? My French isn't that great but doesn't that mean…"

"The Dog House." He laughed softly. "Friends of my parents retired here and he decided to start his own winery. He called his shed the dog house, and that's where it started."

"They'll be closed now," she said. "We can't intrude."

"I called ahead." He glanced over at her. "I want this trip to start out right."

Don't get sucked in too fast, she reminded herself, even as his eyes let her know that he was going to be very busy making love to her as soon as they arrived at their hotel.

This was what happened the last time, she tried to warn her heart. Too much. Too fast. All of it. Too much excitement, too much sex—okay, not too much sex—too intense, maybe. And they'd talked—especially her. She'd talked too much. Given it all away. Everything she thought, hoped, dreamed. Everything she was.

She couldn't do that again, not and risk her heart. So she had to be careful. Right. She was warned, armed, she knew what she was getting into. She did. This time she'd go slower, not put herself out there so much.

The Rosenthals, Ed and Bert (for Bertina, she discovered) were waiting for them. While they poured, Ed described each wine, with candid comments like, "This chardonnay tasted like cat piss the first year. I think we're getting the hang of it now, though." They all tasted good to her. Dennis had the vocabulary and was able to talk wine without sounding like a pompous ass, something she considered almost impossible to pull off.

When they left, the Rosenthals pressed two bottles on them, and added another for Dennis's parents. "You come back and see us next time you two are coming this way. Come stay with us."

"They think we're a couple," she said, as they trudged back to the car.

Dennis didn't say anything, merely picked up her hand and kissed her palm. She had to give herself another quick lecture about overblown responses.

He still wouldn't tell her where they were going, so she just sat back and enjoyed the ride. She saw a sign for The Zen Station, the ultrachic, hottest place in the valley. If only she'd known two months ago that she was going to make this trip, she thought....

Since she'd pretty much never in her life planned a weekend away two months in advance, she'd never stayed at the inn and spa or eaten in the famed restaurant.

When they drove in, she started to laugh. "I wish. You have to book this place months in advance."

She turned to see if this was a joke and he'd back out again with a big har, har guffaw and head to the closest Sheraton. But no. He was going toward the entrance and slowing the car. "You're kidding, right?"

"No." He looked altogether pleased by her evident shock. "I know a guy, who knows a guy..."

She glanced around her at the simple, Japanese-style grounds, the low buildings and started to laugh. "You brought me to a spa."

He cut the engine and turned to face her, removing his sunglasses so she could see into his eyes. "I remember asking you what market research you'd done. It was all good stuff, still you weren't ever stopping to enjoy the spa experience. Maybe it's time you did." He shrugged. "Since this is mostly a business trip."

She couldn't stop the smile that tugged at her mouth. She was stressed, excited, keyed up, a little freaked and she had to look and act her best for the next few days. She was, in fact, exactly the kind of woman who most needed a spa visit. And it would never have occurred to her to book herself one. She'd have considered it an unnecessary indulgence. Dennis knew better.

He had done this for her.

If he'd been thinking of himself they'd be sitting among vineyards about now in one of the high-end wine-route B&Bs or he'd be pecking her on the cheek as he went out for eighteen holes on a Palmer-designed golf course. He hadn't done either of those things, which he would have loved. He'd booked a spa.

Just for her.

She was so touched she had a misty moment when she couldn't think of a word to say. Instead she kissed him slowly, full on the mouth.

"Come on. We can't be late for our massages."

"Massages?"

"Yep. Since we don't have time for the full-day-at-the-spa experience, I booked you for a massage and facial minispa. We eat later. Okay by you?"

"Of course. And you?"

"I can do a massage. Anything else challenges my manhood."

She laughed. "One day, my friend."

"Hey, if I ever give myself over for a rejuvenating eyebrow wax, you'll be the first person I call."

She muttered a little in Spanish, only to annoy him. One day she was going to put him in her spa for a day, and he'd leave a believer. She was an evangelist of the power of relaxation and bringing out the beauty in everyone, and her spa was her revival tent.

She'd have Dennis not only a convert, but eagerly out spreading the word.

He just didn't know it yet.

"Come on," Dennis said, grabbing their overnight bags and tossing the car keys to the parking valet.

When she walked in, she knew she was going to love this place. It smelled wonderful, like the most subtle incense. The decor was Zen meets Feng Shui with a little L.A. thrown in for the big-shots—ferns, a fountain wall and low, wooden benches. When they reached their room, she let out a squeak of delight. The biggest bed she'd ever seen dominated the room, and a huge French door led to a deck with a view of the valley. The ensuite bathroom was a minispa all its own with a jetted tub made for two, black stones arranged in pots and tiny bottles of products she knew couldn't be quite as good as hers.

"Do we have time for a bath?"

He glanced at his watch. "Not if you want to get to your spa in time."

"Do we have time for a quickie?"

His grin was swift and lethal. "Yep."

Laughing, she threw herself at him, knocking him to the big bed and grabbing at his clothes. They came together fast, uncomplicated and full of magic. The sheets felt like clouds, and the sunshine slanted in through the window, gilding their bodies as they rolled together, thrusting, reaching, gasping, and finally sighing, the long *yessss* of pleasure shared.

"How much time until my appointment?" she asked, stifling the urge to fall asleep with her head on Dennis's chest, the gentle pounding of his heart as lulling as the surf.

"Fifteen minutes."

A quick brush of her lips over his and she ran naked to the bathroom. She was showered, dried and belting one of the luxury robes the color of oatmeal in five minutes. The closet contained spa sandals. How perfect! She put one of the keycards in her pocket and left.

Darn it, she thought, a half hour later as she was drifting pleasantly under the ministrations of a strange woman in a strange spa giving her a facial, Dennis was right. It was good for her to enjoy a spa as a guest.

She always told her clients that part of the benefit they were receiving was simple relaxation, in an age where she didn't know a single woman—except perhaps her *abuela,* who took her siesta every afternoon—who bothered to take time to rest. Who took time for themselves? Everyone was so busy, with careers, sports, kids, their schedules, their kids' schedules, fund-raising, consciousness raising, marathon racing—sometimes it seemed that no one in California, perhaps in the modern world, was ever still. Here, lying with her eyes closed and cucumber slices—clichéd but soothing—over her lids, no sound other than the shhh of the facial steamer, the rustle of the aesthetician's smock and her own breathing, she started to relax.

Relaxed. In spite of her big week of searching for the right location, negotiating for the best rates, she was, at this moment, as relaxed as she'd been in a long time. Between the gorgeous drive, the sexual release, the fun of being somewhere so luxuriously peaceful and the fact of lying here, being pampered, she was taking a first-class minibreak from her hectic life. No wonder spas were a growth industry.

By the time she returned to the room, she was limp as wilted lettuce from the hot stone massage and the merlot-grape facial. She felt so good it seemed mildly sinful. Dennis wasn't in the room—having his own massage, no doubt. She didn't even bother to remove her robe, simply pushed the spa sandals off her feet and flopped facedown onto the bed. She was asleep in a second.

As Dennis entered the room, he was thinking a spa massage wasn't anything he'd ever make fun of again. He carried a lot of tension in his shoulders, his massage lady had told him, as she unwound knots he wouldn't have known he'd tied if he hadn't felt the relief as they gave way to her strong fingers.

Funny how all that pampering could tire a person out, not to mention the killer week as he'd tried to cram two weeks of work into one. Worth it, he thought as he stared down at the sleeping form of his favorite—if pain-in-the-ass—client.

Going on the adage if you can't beat them, join them, he flopped down beside Mercedes. He'd have liked to snuggle up behind her naked, her robe was in the way, though, and he didn't want to wake her. Her breathing was deep and even, more like a woman in a coma than one having a nap. She didn't even stir as he shucked his own robe and wrapped himself around her. When he slipped his fingers down the vee of her robe, and cupped the warm, silky globe of her breast, she sighed and shifted, teasing his palm with her nipple.

Her hair was clipped up, to keep it out of the way, no doubt, and she hadn't bothered to take it down. He put his lips on the column of her long, elegant neck, breathing in her scent, and that of the spa oils they'd used on her. It made her smell slightly foreign, then he breathed again and found her. The scent he'd carry with him forever as the most evocative of fragrances.

"I love you," he said softly.

She shifted again. "Love you," she said, so sleepy she couldn't possibly know how she'd given herself away. He knew, and his lips curved against her skin as he drifted into sleep.

He woke suddenly, not knowing what had wakened him or, for a moment, where he was. The echoes of a heartfelt moan sifted around him until he recognized the sound as his, and a second later groaned again as he realized what had woken him.

Her lips. On his chest, moving slowly down, over his belly. "Mercedes," he groaned. "What are you doing?"

She glanced up at him, her lips tilted in a sensuous invitation. "I thought I should wake you up so you don't miss dinner."

"Can I trade my alarm clock for you?" he managed, before her low laugh echoed against his belly, her mobile mouth kept moving south, and he was lost.

She loved him she'd said. Okay, it was sleepy and she could have been dreaming of Antonio Banderas or

Ricky Martin or some other Latin lover type for all he knew. He didn't think so. In the courtroom of his mind, her unconscious was a witness for his side. She might argue that she was indifferent to him, wanted him mainly for recreation—as well as his sharp legal mind— yet he liked to think her sleepy confession was as true as the admissions made during hypnosis, when the mind bypassed its inhibitions.

The way he'd tell her right now that he loved her if he wasn't inhibited by the suspicion that such an avowal would screw up his second chance with this woman as badly as his insensitivity had screwed it up the first time.

Instead he gave himself over to the sensations, her mouth on him, her hair—newly released he noted— drifting over him, tickling, caressing, stroking. Her hands were so sure. Her mouth a gift.

When he couldn't stand any more, he pulled her up, flipped her, and did back to her what she'd been doing to him. Okay, so his hair didn't do anything much, his hands weren't as soft and they didn't spend all day pampering people, and his mouth tended to take a more direct route to where he wanted to go, still she wasn't complaining.

Her hips lifted when he cupped her with his hands, and she opened to him like an exotic bloom to sunshine. Not a rose. Something more earthy, more tropical and lush. Not an orchid, that was too Georgia O'Keeffe. He bet there was a flower growing in Mexico that would be a match. One day, he'd find it.

Meanwhile, he stroked her petals with his tongue, teasing the center until she was wet and hot and panting, as ready to burst as he. He took her over the edge, feeling the ripples begin under her skin, tasting her passion as her hips began to writhe. He kept at her, softening his strokes until she was limp in his arms, sighing softly, then he rose over her. When he entered her, when their bodies met and melded, he'd never known a more perfect moment.

He wanted to remember everything about it. The way the last rays of sunshine slanted through the big window. The sound of her panting sighs, the feel of the outrageously luxurious sheets against their skin, the smell of herbs and flowers and natural essences or whatever the spa people had used on them, and the sight of her glorious body, moving with his. Even though her first passion was spent, he knew her, knew there was plenty more where that came from, and sure enough, once he started to move, she wrapped her legs around him and thrust up and against him until her head went back and she cried out again. He could hold out, he could. He could bring her up one more time, but they had all night ahead of them.

He figured they'd better pace themselves, so he kissed her, a big, wet, heartfelt kiss that said all the things she wasn't ready to hear, and then he followed her into paradise.

Dinner was predictably spalike. A lot of things from the sea, as if anything marine was somehow superior. Everything seemed to be seasoned with sea salt from France. Seaweed-wrapped sushi, halibut in a no-butter sauce made with some nut he'd just bet grew seventy fathoms beneath the sea. Enough vegetarian options that he assumed his desire for a juicy red steak would be treated as a joke. In the end he went for the halibut, which was surprisingly good. Not that it mattered what was on his plate.

All his attention, all his senses, were on the woman in the black dress sitting across from him. The dress had a silk band that stretched across her lush breasts, making him long to dip his fingers into it and touch her. She wore gold hoop earrings and a gold necklace with a big round of polished rock. Jade maybe, or turquoise. Her hair was down, the way he liked it, and she was not only the most beautiful, but the most dynamic woman in the restaurant.

Her hand rested on the stem of her water glass. He reached over and toyed with her fingers. "Glad I came along?"

"No. I wish my uncle Herb was here instead. Have you ever seen my uncle Herb in a belching contest? He cleans up."

He chuckled. "Okay, so I was fishing for a compliment. A nice, 'Oh, Dennis, I'm so happy you're here. I'm so glad we're back together,' would soothe my fragile ego."

"There's nothing wrong with your ego." There was a tiny smile tilting her lips that told him she was glad he was with her.

"So, tell me about your uncle Herb. Does he really exist?"

"Sure. He's my dad's brother. He's…exactly what you'd think a guy who wins belching contests would be like. Worked in a pulp mill for years. He's what you might call a rough diamond."

"You never talk about your father's family." He glanced up at her. "Well, you never talk about your father."

She shrugged. "Not much to tell. He left when I was ten. He was an okay father. He went to work, came home, was assistant coach on my brother's baseball team. Then I think he got tired of being grown-up and responsible. His exotic Mexican beauty of a wife wasn't such a beauty anymore and had turned into a big nag. So he found somebody else. It's not an unusual story."

"And he broke your heart."

She snorted and pulled her fingers out of his reach. "Please. He didn't even break Mama's heart. They were mostly fighting all the time by then." Her face had the taut look of a mask. Did she think he couldn't see the hurt and pain behind it? Why wouldn't she let him in?

She glanced at him under her lashes. "My temper comes from my mother's side."

"Is her aim as good?" He touched the side of his head where the candle rocket had burned a chunk of his hair.

"Better. Where do you think my brother got his baseball arm?"

By the time they were eating the fresh fruit dessert, and he figured there were so many vitamins, minerals and free-radical-fighting agents in his system that he ought to be able to live on chips and beer for the rest of his life and get away with it, he admitted he wanted more from Mercedes.

More than the sprightly small talk she'd bounced to the second she grew uncomfortable talking about her past.

When they left the dinner table, he suggested a walk.

The grounds were magnificent in that better-than-nature-intended, resort-grounds way.

He took her hand as they stepped out and began crunching along gravel paths, meandering among the ferns and lilies. The lap pool glowed like an opal, lit from within with floodlights. Palm trees and wild orchids lined the paths. He could smell the fat, dark-leaved bushes that must have been chosen for their aromatherapeutic properties as well as their blossoms.

He wanted to know more about the woman beside him. Wanted to know everything. The way she'd talked about her father at dinner had amazed him. He couldn't believe that in their three wild months together, he'd learned so little of what really mattered to her. Sure, he'd known her parents were divorced. It was California, after all, not exactly a rarity. He hadn't suspected until tonight how much it had affected her.

"I'm sorry your dad left you like that," he said softly.

He felt her stiffen, all the way to the fingertips linked with his.

"Happens all the time."

This was only now hitting him. "Your mom's family is Catholic, right?"

She nodded.

"And, coming from Mexico, pretty traditional I guess."

She nodded again. "It was so humiliating for her. And, of course, then the money got really tight. He could barely afford the home and four kids he had, then he took off and started another family."

"Ouch."

"Yeah. My mom had to go back to work. It was good

for me because I spent so much time in the summer on my grandmother's farm." Her fingers relaxed within his grip and she seemed open to talking. "We could have moved in with my *abuela*. Mom wouldn't do it. That would have been so much worse for her."

"What did your mom do?"

"She retrained as a hairdresser, which meant she could work more flexible hours, since she had four kids. She worked at the salon at a country club."

"Is that how you got started?"

"Yes. I used to come in on weekends and sometimes after school. I swept the floors and washed hair. Stuff like that. But I saw the products they were using, how much they were charging for the services, and I knew I could do better. The creams my grandmother's family made were so much…I don't know. Richer, I guess, and I'd seen how they worked. All they needed was fancy packaging.

"I knew I could make those women look younger. And for the prices they were willing to pay?" She laughed like a winning gambler at Vegas. "I knew right then what I wanted to do."

He dropped a hand on her shoulder. "That took a lot of guts."

"Stupidity, pride, arrogance." She shrugged. "Worked out okay, though.".

"Do you ever see him?"

Her mind was obviously on the spa still, for she turned, and in the moonlight her skin was like gold, her eyes dreamy. "See who?"

"Your father."

The dreamy look faded, and if her skin still glowed,

he couldn't tell since she turned away. "What are you? My shrink? Of course I see him."

"You've never talked about him."

"You and I have never been about talking." The look she sent him went straight to his groin, as she must have known it would. He didn't want to be so easily distracted.

"I want us to do a lot more talking. This is the new and improved us. We can do better, you know."

She kissed him, teasing him with her tongue until he was mindless.

"I've got a big day tomorrow," she said. "We should go to bed."

He wanted to talk to her, to share everything that had ever hurt her or made her laugh or brought her a moment of unexpected joy. He wanted to tell her all the things he'd ever thought about or wanted or dreamed of.

It looked like that wasn't about to happen. Not tonight.

As hot as the sex was, and with them it was always hot, he felt discontented.

For the first time in his life, he got what the big deal was with woman always wanting to talk. Damn it, there was some disturbing role reversal going on here. He wanted to communicate, and all Mercedes wanted was sex.

The whole thing made him irritable. Was he just being used for his body?

10

"How do I look?" Mercedes asked anxiously, swiveling in the mirror so she could see herself from all sides, searching for loose threads, dog hair, any mar or imperfection in her linen suit.

"You look great," Dennis assured her, as he turned from the mirror where he was knotting his tie. His gaze warmed as it ran over her. "Sexy. A corporate barracuda."

She grinned, delighted that he'd caught on right away that she needed to project strength and power, since she felt like such a fraud inside.

"Don't forget that you are the customer. They want to kiss your ass."

She smoothed her skirt once more. "I'm saving that job for you."

She didn't even have to ask him to keep the top up in the convertible. He understood without being lectured that her hair, makeup and clothing needed to stay unmussed.

They drove away from the resort and she glanced back, wondering if they'd ever come here again.

"So, what are the specs on this first place?" he asked.

She took out the paper-clipped bundle Camilla had prepared and told him. "This one's in a retail complex."

"A mall?"

"No. Sort of a strip mall. Very high end, though. A couple of designer clothing stores, one of those grocery markets where everything's organic and the olive oil hasn't even been pressed. It's been coaxed."

"Got it."

"The space used to be a spa. Now it's empty. The challenge, of course, is running a successful spa in spaland. Then again, that's why people come to Calistoga."

The real estate agent who was supposed to meet them never showed up. In the end it didn't matter. She didn't like the location, no wonder it had gone belly up. The town itself was wonderful. She could smell the sulphur from the springs in the air. The small town was all about food and wine and mud baths. It was charming, quaint and somehow not for her.

"Robert Louis Stevenson spent his honeymoon just north of here, you know," Dennis said as they sipped takeout coffees and waited for the agent.

"I bet he wasn't the last."

Dennis glanced at his watch. "Want me to rustle up the agent?"

"No. It's not for me."

He nodded. "Okay." He opened the car door for her and she skipped inside.

"One down, six to go."

"And that's just the A list. There are probably twenty properties on the B list."

"I'm an A-list girl only."

"Fair enough. What's next?" he asked as they pulled out.

"Two in the Sacramento area. The first one is fourteen thousand square feet. Bigger than my current space. That's a plus. I could add more features."

"Area demographics?"

"Upscale. Mainly thirty to sixties, nice median income in the area, with a number of working women who would love to come to my spa." She read on and said, "Ah, I remember now, there's a wedding shop and planner in the complex. We could do some joint promotions and advertising." She glanced over at Dennis and grinned. "Bridal parties love spas."

"Sounds good. What are the negatives?"

"Parking's going to be an issue, and Camilla had a question about the traffic flow pattern off the main roads." She shook her head. "If the place is hard to get to and a pain to park in, clients will hate it."

When they reached the site, she knew almost immediately that it was wrong. The empty space had been an exercise equipment retailer that had gone bankrupt. After waiting almost five minutes before there was a break in the traffic to get into the lot, then driving around to secure a space, she and Dennis glanced at each other and nothing more needed to be said.

"Let's go inside, anyway, now we're here," he said. "We made an appointment."

"I agree."

The leasing agent, a high-pressure type, directed his entire sales pitch to Dennis. He was probably twenty-five, with styled hair and a habit of creasing his forehead to try to look older. After five minutes Dennis stopped the guy midsentence. "It's not me you want to talk to, it's my boss."

The agent laughed. "Yeah, man. I know. My wife's the boss, too."

She bet he wasn't even married.

Dennis merely shook his head. "Ms. Estevez is not my wife. She owns the spa. I'm her lawyer." He sent Mercedes the ghost of a wink. "Part of her acquisition team."

"Right. Ah—"

"And we're not interested," Mercedes said. "Thank you anyway.

"What a loser," she said, when they were back on the road. "At least he made it easy to leave in a hurry."

The second stop was a real contender, the ground floor of an office/residential complex that offered lots of parking, easy access and a quiet area. The down side was the price was the highest. The owner of the building met them and showed them around. He was a courtly older European man. German, she was guessing from the slight accent.

After they'd spent time wandering the twelve-thousand-foot space, and she mentally laid out the various stations, it was close to one o'clock. Their host said, "Would you join me for lunch? The restaurant is next door. It will give you a feel for the building."

Dennis raised his eyebrows to her in a silent question, and she nodded, so they waited while the owner locked up, and then the three of them walked to a bistro-style restaurant doing a busy lunch trade. Mercedes noted a number of working women who could use her services and certainly looked as though they could afford them.

She knew from Camilla's research notes that the area was a mix of high- and medium-income residential with a number of high-tech and financial buildings. Ideal.

She also liked their host, who turned out to be Polish. Not that Poland was anywhere near Mexico. They did, however, share the common experience of being immigrants to America. Henry Gorzinsky charmed her and she did her best to charm him right back.

Dennis felt as though he were at a supper club. Along with a very nice blackened monkfish on organic salad greens, he was able to enjoy himself as Mercedes and her new conquest flattered each other. Gorzinsky was trying to decide if he wanted the spa and if Mercedes could make a success of it if he did. Mercedes, unless he was seriously wrong, was interested yet not totally sold on the space and wanted a break on the rent.

Whatever happened, he was bound to enjoy the next hour.

Gorzinsky managed to throw anecdotes into the conversation that concerned groups of women who worked in the building, a number of wealthy widows who owned homes in the complex and various other tidbits that would no doubt appeal to Mercedes's business instincts.

She, on the other hand, managed to slide in a few facts of her own, such as the parts of her family history that involved secret recipes, the ones that had helped make her spa such a success. Sure, she was implying, just any old spa might not work here. Hers definitely would—if she decided on this place.

When the mineral water bottle was empty, their three plates cleaned and coffee was on the table, Mercedes excused herself and went to the washroom.

Mr. Gorzinsky wasted no time. He turned to Dennis and said, the twinkle in his faded-blue eyes gone, "Mr. McClary, I do not like to make mistakes. They are costly and inconvenient. I like that young lady very much. I have to ask myself, does she have the stamina to run two successful enterprises?"

Dennis decided he liked his host for being honest enough to raise what was on his mind. "Mr. Gorzinsky. I'm here as part of Ms. Estevez's acquisition team. I'm hardly going to undermine her in her absence." They'd been "Mercedes" and "Henry" all over the place, still he preferred the slight distance of formality.

The older man regarded him for an uncomfortable moment when Dennis felt as if he was under a microscope. "You are also in love with her. That much is plain, my dear sir."

Dennis choked on the water he was drinking but didn't bother arguing. What would be the point? He merely made a sound that could have been yes, no, that's none of your damn business, or I am so in love with that woman it hurts.

Gorzinsky continued. "A man who loves a woman doesn't want her to make a misstep."

"I think…" He sipped more water to give himself time to articulate the truth as he knew it. "I think that Mercedes has the talent, the brains and the ambition to be the next Estée Lauder." Even as he said it, he felt how exciting her future could be. He had a mental image of her face on a billboard, a television ad. "She's one in a million. She's got what it takes to become a brand. She's beautiful, smart—" he cocked an eyebrow "—you've seen her charm at work. And clients love her and her products. I think we're seeing the start of something very exciting. She's an amazing woman."

"Such a woman is not easy for a man to love."

Dennis was startled. How had they gone from forecasting sales per square foot to his future love life. "Oh, believe me, she's very easy to love."

"You misunderstand. For a man, a woman who is more successful can be a great wound to the pride. She will have the limelight and he will be the one in the shadow. Are you prepared for that?"

Dennis chuckled. "You've been in California too long, Mr. Gorzinsky. Everybody ends up as an amateur therapist here."

"I speak from experience. I loved an opera singer in Berlin. I spent several years in her shadow. Such a voice. Such a star." He was quiet for a moment and Dennis imagined him reliving the heady days.

"What happened?"

"I was indispensable to her. I carried her wrap, opened doors, made certain the foreign press spelled her name correctly and that no one put the wrong flowers in her dressing room or annoyed her in any way when she had to perform. It is not an easy role for a man of pride and with his own sense of ambition."

"Did you make it work?"

Mr. Gorzinsky smiled, but his eyes were sad. "We

were married for thirty years. She died of a brain tumor, two years past."

"It was worth it then?"

"True love always is."

MERCEDES HAD NO IDEA what the two men had talked about behind her back. Whatever it was, they sure seemed chummy when she returned. Over coffee, they talked about weather, California politics, Mr. Gorzinsky's grandchildren and Dennis, who'd been reticent during the first part of the lunch, joined in as though he and their host had been friends for years.

When they left, with expressions of mutual regard and a promise to be in touch, Mr. Gorzinsky surprised her by kissing her on both cheeks, very Euro, very charming. As he brushed her right cheek, he said softly, "That young man loves you very much. Hang on to him."

She was so startled her jaw about dropped to her knees. Love? Dennis and she had never, ever used those words. She didn't know what to say, so she said nothing.

She watched Dennis's turn at goodbye. He got a manly handshake and definitely no whispered message.

How bizarre was that?

"What did you and Henry talk about when I was in the ladies'?" she finally asked when they were once more on the highway, the sun casting long shadows. They'd been at lunch longer than she'd realized.

"Honestly? He asked me if I thought you had what it takes to make a success of two spas."

If she could take back her question, she realized, she'd do it right now. There was a weird, hollow feeling in her chest. She didn't know if she was interested in the answer. Of course, Dennis was her lawyer, and he'd come as her friend and lover, too. Still that didn't mean he believed in her. Not all-the-way believed.

She forced a carefree tone to her voice and tilted back her head to look up at the sky. "That was a sneaky move, asking about me behind my back."

Out of the corner of her eye she saw Dennis glance her way. "Don't you want to know what I said?"

She squeezed her eyes shut behind her sunglasses, something she used to do when she wished on a new moon or birthday cake candles. "Only if it's good."

She felt the car sway and her eyes flew open, then they were bumping to the side of the road and pulling to a stop.

Dennis turned to her. "I told him that you are the real deal, lady." He sounded a little awed as though what he was saying was a surprise to him. "I told him that you are going to be huge. A woman so powerful she's her own brand, like Martha Stewart or Estée Lauder."

"You should have said Helena Rubenstein. She was from Eastern Europe, too. Henry would have appreciated that." She remained outwardly cool; inside joy was bubbling like lava. She wanted to say something else, something about how important it was that he believed in her, because that helped her believe in herself, yet she couldn't do it. It sounded borderline needy, and a guy could get the feeling that she cared more than she was willing to admit.

Besides, Henry's whispered suggestion that she hold on to Dennis had freaked her right out.

Dennis was for fun. Love was way too serious.

A monster RV rumbled by, it was white with black writing, she noticed. One of those rental ones for tourists. She imagined a family from Alaska or Maine or Sweden staring at the couple pulled over on the side of the road in the convertible, holding hands. They'd think they'd had a fight and were making up, or maybe that the man was proposing.

Whoa. That Polish matchmaker had really shaken her up.

Dennis squeezed her hands. "It was the weirdest thing. I was sitting there, telling him how amazing you are, and I got this...I don't know what to call it. Sort of a vision. I could see you on a billboard, or on a television ad."

"How did I look?"

"Like Catherine Zeta-Jones, only sexier."

"You're crazy."

"I'm telling you, I believe in you. I think you can go all the way with this thing."

His utter belief in her had her heart thumping as the thrill of what he was saying sank in. She'd imagined herself countless times, in truth, doing those very things. She'd read too many motivational books not to know all about visualization. Spooky that Dennis was seeing her success in the same way, and as clearly.

Two pairs of motorcyclists roared by. They were seniors enjoying retirement. And why not?

"You're not saying anything."

"I don't know what to say. I'm...I'm really happy you believe in me." No, that wasn't enough. She drew in a breath. "It means a lot."

The wind whipped a tendril of hair into her face, and before she could reach for it, Dennis tucked it behind her ear. "I want to be there for you. Help you go as far as you can."

He looked so serious, and beneath her excitement was barely acknowledged fear. He was trying to get her to move beyond where she was ready to go. So she did what she always did when he confused her. She kissed him, and then she slipped her hand down his nice tie, over the nicely defined chest, and the flat stomach, coming to rest lightly over the bulge in his pants.

"I think we should go all the way," she whispered, teasing into his ear.

To her shock, he removed her hand and put it back in her lap.

"I know you're scared. I think I'm finally starting to understand you. I love making love with you and playing your games more than I've ever enjoyed another woman…. I'm more than that." He yanked off his glasses and looked unexpectedly fierce. "We're more than that."

He'd chided her and maybe she deserved it. Still, it stung. "Maybe I don't want more than that."

"All men don't leave, Mercedes, even if you try and push them away. The right man will stay."

11

MERCEDES WAS FURIOUS. How dare he? Here they were pulled over on the highway while the whole world drove by, and he was talking about being the right man.

"I don't need a man. Everything I've done has been on my own." A semi drove by in an explosion of sound, giving her an excuse to shout. "I don't need anyone."

"Of course you don't," he shouted back. "This isn't about need."

"Then what is it about?"

He put his sunglasses back on, signaled and pulled into the traffic. Only when they were cruising the highway once more did he bother to answer her. "I guess you're going to have to figure that out for yourself."

Time went by like the road beneath their wheels, and finally he said, "Well? What did you think of that space?"

She was relieved to have him change the subject. "I liked it. I liked Henry. I think it could work." She described the layout as she'd envisioned it, and his comments were astute and thoughtful. Their little tiff might never have happened.

"And Sacramento's a manageable distance from San Francisco, so you can keep an eye on both places."

bed." She laughed. "For the first month I thought you didn't drink coffee."

"It's funny, but I don't feel that same urgency this time around."

"That's because we're on a road trip. You have access to my body 24/7." She regarded him with her head tilted as though he were a new species she'd never encountered before. "No. It isn't that."

"Maybe," he reached over to play with the tip of her ponytail where it lay in dark, glossy strands against her T-shirt, "it's because this time we're both wondering if it's more."

She opened her mouth, her head already starting to shake in what could only be denial. He put a finger over her lips, silencing her. "I'm asking you to open your mind to the possibility that there's more between us than sex," he said. "That's all I ask."

For a moment they remained motionless, his finger still on her mouth. He felt the soft warmth of her lips, her breath against his finger as she breathed out, the sun had set and night shadows puddled around them.

She was gazing at him through those brilliant brown eyes but not giving him a whole lot of clue as to what she was thinking.

He took his finger away and still felt the imprint of her lips, like a kiss. There was a tiny crease in her forehead, and he could sense her uncertainty before she spoke. "I have so much going on right now."

"Hey," he said, hoping to reassure her. "I'm not asking for anything except that you allow the new and improved us to go wherever it's going. Fair enough?"

She smiled, looking relieved. What was she expecting? A marriage proposal? He, too, was hesitant about their future; at least he was willing to believe they could have one.

"Let's go to bed," he said.

She nodded and they rose together.

The night air was still warm. He liked her long stride in sneakers. Not that he didn't love her legs in high heels, nevertheless their strides matched this way, and they walked in comfortable silence. Her hand felt warm and right tucked into his. He felt like one big happy face. Dennis, the human smile. When she turned to him, he thought he'd say something romantic or sexy, then she frowned. "What am I doing? Am I insane?" Her voice was tinged with panic.

If she considered that even thinking about the possibility of a real relationship was insane, then their future as a couple didn't look bright. However, he swallowed his hasty retort. He was a lawyer. Trained to get the facts before taking a position. So, instead of telling her that, yeah, she was insane if she was going to panic about finding someone who really cared about her, he said, "Tell me what's going on in that head?"

"Dennis, I'm twenty-eight years old, everything I know about business I learned from night school and watching *The Apprentice* on TV. I'm going to have to borrow a ton of money to get this second spa up and running." She gulped like a downed surfer coming up for air. "Maybe I've got ideas that are too big for where I am. And who I am."

"Do you really believe that?"

She smiled wryly. "Some days."

A cool breeze lifted the palm fronds and set them to whispering overhead. It brought the scent of the sea and the bickering of seagulls. "I meant what I said in the car. I think you are amazing and you can do anything you want."

"There's nothing wrong with running one spa, and doing a good job of it, is there?"

"No." He glanced at her, so solemn beside him, a rare expression of uncertainty on her face. She hid her insecurities so well most of the time, that, once again, he'd missed the signs. "Is that what you want?"

Her head fell back as though she were going to abandon conversation for star gazing, or that the answer to his question would be printed on one of those banners that small planes fly across the sky. Instead of Marry me, Rosemary, or Two for One Pizza, she'd see Play it Safe, or Shoot for the Stars. Maybe he hadn't known her long, but he was certain he knew what she really wanted. Sure enough, she said, "No. I want the second location this year. Two more next year. Exactly as planned."

"You know, it's good to be scared."

"It is?"

"Yep. It stops you doing anything really stupid."

"Do you think this expansion is stupid?"

"No. I'd have tried to stop you if I thought that, not come along for the ride."

There was a tiny silence before she said. "Oh. Good."

When they got back to the hotel, the lobby was a zoo, with a snaking line of people all trying to check out at the same time. She could feel the crackle of tempers barely held, see feet tapping and wristwatches being consulted. The desk clerks looked frantic.

"Glad we're not trying to check in now."

"Or out."

"I wonder what's going on," she said, and he pointed to one of those TV screen things with the hotel events listed. A big telecom convention ended today.

They rode up to their room and walked down the hall past two exhausted-looking women dragging a hotel cart, speaking softly in Spanish. "Still cleaning rooms?" Mercedes asked them in their own language.

"Sí," the older one said, putting a hand to her back where it obviously ached. Everyone had checked out from the convention at the same time. They still had two more rooms to finish before they could go home.

"I hope you'll be finished soon," she said with sympathy.

"Gracias." And smiling at Dennis, they both said, *"Buenos tardes."*

They entered their room and she said, "Okay if I head straight for the shower?"

"Sure. I'll check e-mail. Maybe flick a few channels."

"No porn," she warned him.

"You never let me have any fun."

She pulled her hair free, shaking her head to loosen it. Right before she shut the bathroom door, she heard Dennis call. "Mercedes. Could you come out here for a minute please?" He sounded…odd.

"What?"

She marched out to find him staring at her with an expression on his face she knew well. It was the way he looked at her right before they fell into bed. Hungry, intent, erotic.

"I need to shower."

"No porn, she says." He shook his head at her. "What, did you bribe the maids to leave us a few props?"

"What are you talking about? You're a madman." She marched over to him, trying very hard not to respond to that look she knew so well.

He gestured. A lawyer presenting Exhibit A to the jury.

There was an ice cube tray with the ice half-melted on the bedside table sitting next to the television remote. She was about to remind him that those poor maids were totally overworked with that convention checking out, when she realized there was more than ice that had scooped her roommate's attention.

The red-and-yellow tiebacks from the curtains were in the middle of the bed instead of being hooked up.

She turned at last to face him and in spite of herself started to feel majorly turned on.

"You bribed those nice women to leave these sex toys out, didn't you?" he said softly.

She threw back her head and laughed, a deep laugh that shook her to her toes. "Melting ice cubes and curtain ties are sex toys?"

He stepped closer. "You speak Spanish. You seemed awfully friendly with those ladies," he said, fighting a grin.

She shook her head. "You're right. You've got me. The maids and I were discussing the various and exquisite uses of ice on a hot female—or male—body, oh, and bondage as practiced in Latin America."

He must know that it was total coincidence that the

poor maids had left these couple of things undone, still her temperature rose and her shower was forgotten. Dennis was the only man she'd ever known who made sex this much fun. He reached out, almost lazily, and scooped a shiny, wet cube into his fingers.

"It was a great idea," he said, reaching forward and sliding the cold wetness over the slope of her breast, where the skin was bare, and rubbing it onto the T-shirt fabric and right over her bulging nipple.

12

THE SKIN WHERE he'd touched her was wet and textured with goose bumps, her nipple the mother of all goose bumps.

She didn't answer, unless a faint sigh counted. The ice was cold against his fingers, the surrounding feeling of her skin was warm bordering on hot. He liked the combination. He got the distinct feeling she did, too. He didn't stay in one place long enough for the cold to get uncomfortable, he kept the ice in motion until droplets of water glistened across her upper chest and slid down to disappear between her breasts. Then he dried his wet hand by running it down over the T-shirt. He could feel her heart pounding and hear the short breaths she was taking. She sounded incredibly aroused for so little action. He loved how quick and responsive her body was.

"What do you think I'd want with a couple of curtain ties?" he asked her. He reached for one and her eyes widened. He gripped it, flexing it between his hands. "Nice heft." He reached out and ran the blue-and-gold-striped cord down her arm, curling it around her wrist.

He'd never been a big fan of bondage; he liked to

have everybody's hands roaming and touching whatever they felt like touching, especially when it was Mercedes's hands. He hated to put them out of commission; then again, the idea of having her helpless, of taking total control, would add spice to their encounter.

Having her helpless beneath him while he pleasured her seemed like a pretty good plan.

"You didn't plan to tie me up, did you?"

"N-no," she said, her body sending off waves of heat that belied her stuttered negative.

"Well then," he said, leaning in to kiss her, "I guess you were right."

"I'm not big on the, um, the bondage thing," she said haltingly.

"Uh-huh. Can you lift your arms for me, honey?"

She did, and as he slid the T-shirt over her head she said, from inside the T-shirt, "I'm not used to giving up control, you see."

He was glad her eyes were covered so she couldn't see his smile. "Sometimes trying new things is good for you."

"What are you doing?"

"I'm helping you out of your shorts."

"Shouldn't you finish taking my T-shirt off?"

He let the shorts slide straight to the floor and then stood back. "No. I think I got the order right."

Her arms were over her head, the shirt covering her from the neck up. Beneath that, her breasts almost tumbled out of the sports bra, her nipples like gold nuggets.

Her belly was long and lean, and a pair of sensible cotton panties that matched the bra hung low on her hips. Nice long legs. There was a small scar on her upper thigh. How had he never noticed that before? He wondered how she'd come by it.

"Where did you get this scar?" he asked, touching it. As though she couldn't stop herself, she eased her legs open a little wider. "I was climbing a tree and I fell out."

"Tomboy, huh?"

"I was seventeen. I was climbing out of my window to meet a boy."

He scooped another wet ice cube. She didn't ask him his intentions so he didn't tell her. It was funny, he wasn't into bondage, and he hadn't intended to use the curtain cord to tie her up, then here she was with her T-shirt nearly blindfolding her and binding her arms, and he liked it very much. From the lack of complaints or struggles, he had to figure Mercedes liked it, too.

Since taking off her bra would involve getting the T-shirt off first, he pulled the bra down so her breasts sat perkily over top. Nice. He warmed a nipple up with his mouth and then rubbed it with the ice.

"Oh," she gasped, arching against the hot and cold. "Oh."

He warmed the cold, jutting nipple with his mouth one more time, unable to resist putting the ice to her other breast, warm and cold, back and forth. She was squirming and so turned on he could feel her arousal. Some little drops of water, cool, then rapidly warmer, slid down her belly. He followed one with his tongue to the point where it was absorbed by her panties. He tasted the salt of her run on her skin, smelled the clean sweat.

He'd had enough of those panties. Hooking his thumbs into the waistband, he eased them down her legs. Her curls were a rich chestnut color, glossy in the light. He didn't ask her to step out of her panties, simply tugged on one shoe until she raised her foot. He dug around for more ice, scooping three cubes. He pressed one against the upper slope of her ass and while she was busy gasping as he rubbed the coldness over her cheeks, he popped the other cubes into his mouth. He pressed his mouth against her intimate curls and blew cold, moist air against her.

"Oh, n-yah!" He felt the flesh on her ass ripple with cold, and he felt the heat of her so close to his mouth. Hot and cold. Cold and hot. He licked her. Starting from the hot, wet opening of her body which was salt-sweet and slick, trailing up to her clit which was swollen hard. Like she was about to burst. Oh, he knew how that felt.

With the tip of his tongue he swirled and licked until her hips started to buck against him, then he withdrew and held his tongue against the ice for a moment. When he touched her clit again with the tip of his tongue she sucked in a breath.

"That's cold, so cold, ohhh." She didn't sound as if she was complaining, and with his cheeks chipmunked with ice, he wasn't in a position to ask. His mouth was filling with cold water and she was so hot she was going to blow any second. He tipped her back so she toppled onto the bed on her back, he pushed his head between her legs and let the cold water wash over her mound.

She squealed and giggled and squirmed. There was a small chunk of ice left, like a smooth stone, and he used his tongue to push it right up inside her. Then he pulled her clit into his mouth and showed her every trick he'd ever learned with his tongue.

He felt the moment when she hovered on the edge, her woman's parts so swollen and hard they felt like barely ripe fruit. Above him she'd thrashed around so much that the T-shirt had pulled right over her head, which was thrown back. Her hair was a tossing tangle, her cries hoarse. He wanted to take her. He wanted to be inside her when she came, yet he also wanted to suck the orgasm right out of her. She was slick and hot and her plump flesh richly flushed as though painted with wine. It throbbed to the frantic pulse of her heart.

One more time he teased her with a long, thorough stroke of his tongue, and then, when she was almost airborne, he grabbed hold of the hips that she'd thrust at him and gave her what she needed, tonguing her until she exploded in a long, sobbing release.

She was trembling all over when she finally came down and he couldn't stop kissing her, her still-throbbing lips, her shaking thighs, her knees.

She pulled off the T-shirt and her bra and glanced down at him. For the first time she looked a little embarrassed. "You aren't even undressed."

"Give me three seconds."

He made it in two.

Her gaze scanned his body as eagerly as he'd watched her. Her smile told him she approved, and he felt like a fool to be so pleased about it.

She reached forward to touch his eagerly jutting cock, and for an awful moment when she wrapped her warm and still-shaky hand around him, he thought he might blow. "I think I need a minute," he told her, gently pulling her wrist.

"I think I need you inside me," she said.

The ice cube tray was empty except for a few small puddles of water. He was going to tip those maids like they'd never been tipped before.

Grabbing a condom, he ripped the package open with his teeth. He was ready in a second. She'd moved away from the wet spot she and the ice water had made between them, so she was half sitting with her back against the pillows. She was totally, gorgeously buck naked. "You know," he said, pulling her legs so they flopped open over his, "you have the nicest body I've ever been privileged to see."

"Thank you. I feel the same about you."

"Really? Can I put it inside you now?"

Her lips twitched. "Yes. Please."

He lifted her hips and they both watched as he slid slowly into her body. Oh, it felt like heaven. Hot and juicy, tight enough that he felt the pull and squeeze as she accommodated him.

She stroked his chest and his shoulders, exploring, and he realized he'd missed having her hands on him with her head and arms stuck in that shirt. Her hands were long fingered and sensual, and he liked the feel of them on his chest and belly. He thrust in and out slowly, and she moved gently in time with him. Mostly he was moving slowly to hang on to control. Maybe because things had turned out so unexpected. He'd imagined they'd both shower, maybe watch the news. Make love quietly before sleeping in each other's arms. If she hadn't mentioned watching porn right at the moment he'd glimpsed the ice and the curtain ties, he never would have got so turned on. However, she had, and he had, and sleepy sex after the news was no longer an option.

Slow was good, *good,* he reminded himself, yet slow was right now impossible. When he could stand it no more he pulled her hips down beneath him into good old faithful missionary position and he plunged hard and deep.

Her eyes widened and she cried out as sudden pleasure coursed through her, her head thrown back. He would think he had hurt her if he hadn't seen a smile on her lips that looked both X-rated and very familiar. He kept pulling almost all the way out, holding it for the tiniest moment and then plunging all the way; he seemed to be hitting *G* for the Good spot, the way she was pulling him in and moaning her pleasure. As much as he'd have liked to drag it out all night, some things were beyond a man's control.

When she wrapped her legs around his hips and grabbed his ass, he knew he was a goner. He gave up any semblance of control and bucked like a wild man. A drop of sweat dripped from his face to splash on her shoulder. She didn't notice or care, she was pulling him into her as hard as he was pushing to get there and they were both panting.

"I'm going to—"

She jerked up against him and he felt her climax from inside, one of the greatest feelings in the world. She squeezed, hot and viselike and he was gone.

He felt his climax roll up and burst out of him like fireworks, and his yell was enough to drown out her frantic cries.

His arms were trembling, he noticed, and there was no way he could speak. For a stunned moment they stared at each other, chests heaving and sweat glowing. Then her eyes started to narrow and tilt up at the corners. She didn't have to say, "That was fantastic," it was written in the look in her eyes.

He leaned over and kissed her slowly, feeling softer than soft skin, the fading drumbeat of her heart and the sweet deep kissing of her mouth against his.

Her lips trembled a little, and he thought he could go on kissing her and making love to her forever, never getting out of this bed except to eat room service meals.

She sighed and slipped her arms around his neck, rubbing her breasts against his chest.

The news was forgotten. He had no idea what was going on in the world, and right now he really didn't care.

13

"It's BIGGER," she said, glancing around the empty space. Newly constructed, this possible spa, one of the last on their list, had cement floors, unfinished walls and no ceiling. "Bigger than the other place."

"You're right. This one's fifteen thousand. Too big?"

"I can make it work."

"A more working-class demographic," he said, consulting his notes. "But the area's up-and-coming."

"Closest competition?"

"At least a forty-five-minute drive." This one was a stand-alone building, lots of parking, nice treed area, yet he didn't like it. Something didn't feel right.

They glanced at each other and in that spooky way they had sometimes of communicating without speaking or even seeming to make a move, they telegraphed a mutual pass on this place.

In fifteen minutes they were back on the road.

"Another one bites the dust," she said moodily. "The Monterey space was too cramped, this one's too…"

"Isolated."

"Was that it?" She turned to him. "I'm so glad you came with me," she said as he pulled out into heavy traffic and onto the freeway. "I like having a second opinion and I would have taken twice as long to find these places."

"Also, no offense, remember I'm the better driver."

Her jaw dropped. "Excuse me?"

"Your mind wanders and you forget what you're doing."

"Yours doesn't?"

He shrugged. "I can think about something else and still concentrate on driving. You can't."

"You're right. You are the better driver."

"You can't be good at everything."

"Hmm."

"Know what?"

She glanced at him with suspicion. "What?"

"You're great in bed."

"I know."

"Know what else?"

"What?"

"I'd rather you were great in bed than a good driver."

A smile curved her lips. "Me, too."

The next three places they saw weren't quite right, either. Mercedes knew she'd feel it when she walked into the right space. She'd done her research, Camilla and Dennis had done more. She had loads of stats at her fingertips, filed in the computer and in her paper files. Ultimately, she'd know in her gut when she found the right place.

Henry Gorzinski's building was the closest so far. But there'd been no big buzz of excitement. There'd been a buzz, though. A definite buzz. But was it enough?

She tapped her fingertips against the dashboard in a tattoo. "Camilla did such a great job with the backup research. We must know everything there is to know about these places. By the way, I called her, and to thank her I've invited her to the spa for a full-day treatment when we get back. She's coming in Friday. You know what that means don't you?"

"My dedicated research lawyer is taking a day off." He sounded grumpy, but she thought he was putting it on.

"Not only that. She's going to be a babe, and you'd better notice. If I find the right location, it will be because of her." She was quiet for a moment. "If I find the right location."

"It's like love," he said after a while. "You meet a lot of women. Pretty women, smart women, hot women. When it's love, you just know. A thousand women could go through your life, and then one day one comes along and pow."

She snorted. "You're an expert on love now?"

He sent her a direct look. "I know what I'm talking about."

And out of the blue she felt breathless. The wind was blowing through her hair, ruffling the bows on the sundress she'd worn because she was tired of business suits. How did Dennis do this? One minute they were talking about Camilla getting a new look and finding her a spa and suddenly she had love thrown at her like a pie in the face.

"I can't even find a spa location. I'm not sure I can do love."

"You'll get there," he said in that calm tone, and she

wasn't sure whether he was talking about the spa location or love.

And she didn't feel like asking him to clarify.

SHE WAS TIRED and a little cranky when they got to the hotel that night, a serene-looking place on the water. They checked in, and as they crossed the lobby to the elevators, they passed the hotel convenience store. "I need some toothpaste. I'll meet you upstairs."

"Okay."

"Need anything?"

"No, thanks."

She collected the toothpaste, some mints, and picked up a women's magazine that had a write-up on spas. Nobody ever featured her in these things. One day soon, she promised herself, adding the magazine to her purchases, one day they would.

She rode the elevator to their floor, and walked to their room, then used her keycard. "Hi, honey, I'm home," she said stepping through the door.

The sound of the shower explained the lack of response.

She walked all the way in, shrugged off her jacket and stared.

There was a hanger lying in the middle of the bed. An ordinary wooden hanger clearly from the hotel closet since it had one of those annoying tops that have to be fitted in to the track on the closet rail. Beside it was a tiny bottle of the hotel's body lotion and a two-foot length of red ribbon.

Tiredness and irritation fled as she recalled the fun they'd managed to have with a forgotten ice cube tray and curtain tiebacks. This time, of course, it wasn't over-worked maids that were to blame. There was something deliberately suggestive about the arrangement on the bed.

The drumbeat of lust turned into a full concert as she stared down at those very mundane items and began to wonder what on earth he planned to do with them. On impulse she dug into her bag and pulled out a hot-pink lip gloss with a stick applicator and tossed that casually into the mix on the theory that Dennis should not be allowed to call all the shots in bed. Or at the prebed teasing stage, either.

When he walked out of the bathroom, damp, freshly showered and wearing nothing but a towel, she was sitting in the armchair, with her feet tucked under her, reading her magazine.

Her cheeks started to warm when he leaned over her shoulder, smelling warm and damp, of the hotel soap and shampoo. And all she could think about were those items on his big bed and what they were going to do with them.

"Mercedes?"

Her whole body rippled with sensation, like a wheat field in a soft breeze. "Yes?"

"Could you come here a minute?"

"Of course."

She rose and walked to join him, staring down at the bed. "What is this?" As if he didn't know. He was pointing to the hanger.

"It's a hanger."

"What's it for?"

"Clothes, I imagine." Though with him, and his sex toys, who knew?

"Then you should put some clothes on it." And he crossed very deliberately to the armchair by the window, removed her magazine, placed it on the side table, and sat down, putting one ankle across the opposite knee and settling in.

She traced the wood of the hanger with her index finger. "Which clothes?" It was almost a whisper.

"Let's start with the ones you're wearing." His voice was smooth and warm. Full of promise.

He hadn't bothered to pull the drapes, so he was a dark blur against the bright background of early-evening light. She stared out. Their building was higher than those around it so there was no way anyone could see inside this room unless they buzzed by on a helicopter. Still, the very idea of stripping in front of a window, and being watched by her lover while she did it, was…exciting. She'd never been much of an exhibitionist. Not much of an anything-ist as far as sex went. Maybe she had, deep in her heart, a traditional streak she'd inherited from her Mexican ancestors, but she was every inch a modern American woman.

She liked sex.

She'd liked it from the first time she'd tried it, with a guy who was a couple of years older and had, thankfully, had enough experience to make the event reasonably pleasurable, in spite of the fact that it had hurt a bit. She hadn't loved him, still he'd been a nice guy, and the six months or so that they'd been together were wonderful. Even then, though, she'd been ambitious. While her first lover was terrific on the football field and pretty good in bed, he hadn't been someone she could talk to, someone who had understood her drive.

"Chill," was what he'd mostly say to her. "You need to chill."

Not likely. So, she'd moved on, and there had been other men. They'd varied in their enthusiasm, appetite and prowess, and she'd had a good time with all.

The best time she'd ever had was with Dennis. She knew it was the same with him.

They'd been crazy for each other, wild with lust and heat and need. Wearing each other out. In all those times, they'd rarely bothered with games. Hadn't needed or wanted them. She didn't own handcuffs, porn, erotica, costumes—she didn't even own a vibrator. Which had caused her girlfriends first to bemoan her prudishness and then, when they discovered how easy climax was for her, to wail with jealousy.

And yet, here she was, playing games. Such a silly game, really. Now that Dennis had stepped in and made deliberate use of a few foolish props, she was surprised at how excited this whole thing was making her feel.

So she'd never been an exhibitionist. It didn't mean she couldn't take pleasure in his obvious thrill watching her. Or that she couldn't imagine strangers watching her through that uncurtained window.

Maybe there was something to sexy games after all, she decided as all her attitude went into cocking a hip. "What item of clothing do you want me to start with?"

"Your dress. I like those bows where the straps are tied. I've been wanting to pull them loose all day."

Just the thought that he'd been thinking about this all day boosted her desire a notch. She sent him a little smile and pulled the ribbon of one bow. The spaghetti straps of her sundress fell apart, one to the front and the other tickling her back.

She put a hand to the bodice and pulled the other bow. She let go and the dress danced down her body to curtsy at the floor.

"Nice," he said as though she were a wine he were thinking about buying. But he did love his wine with passion.

Stepping out of the dress, she took the time to retie the bows so the dress would hang properly, and she propped her body into every seductive pose she could manage while she did so.

Her bra was a deceivingly skimpy little thing that kept her nipples under control and the jiggle to a minimum. Deciding both jiggle and nipples were definitely good for right now, she slipped that off next and hung it neatly.

Now she was down to panties. No, not quite. With great fanfare, she removed her watch as though it were a long glove and ceremoniously added that to the hanger.

She heard some shifting going on in the direction of the armchair, and she knew the man watching her wasn't as calm as he'd like her to think.

Deciding to keep him on edge, she turned her back to him and then peeled her panties slowly over her hips and down her legs. Thank you, Pilates, she thought as she got them all the way to her ankles without bending her knees.

"Come here," he said, his voice no longer sounding smooth.

"Should I bring the bottle of lotion?"

"Yes."

"The ribbon?"

"Oh, definitely."

"And the lip gloss?"

There was a heavy pause. "What lip gloss?"

"It's here with the other things. You must have over-bribed the maids. They threw in a little something extra."

Since he didn't say anything, she scooped up all the items and took them to him. She felt his eyes on her the whole way.

When she got to where he was sitting, she put the things on the small table beside the chair and said, "Raise your hands."

"I thought I was in charge here."

"You thought wrong."

"I learned a long time ago always to do what a naked woman tells me," he said putting his hands in the air.

"Smart guy. Towel." She unwrapped him, because she felt like it and it made him seem like a gift, which in many ways he was.

There was all this emotional stuff between them. The words he'd implied, the way she'd thrown up barriers to stall him, and yet, somehow she felt that their bodies were doing a lot of communicating. The way she wanted him now was more than merely sexual. What had begun as desire had turned into yearning.

Maybe this togetherness trip had been a bad idea, and yet, she thought, as they touched each other, skin on skin, if she could go back and do this without him, she wouldn't.

"You know what I want you to do with that ribbon?" he asked, pointing to the silky red snake.

"What?"

"I want you to tie your hair back so I can watch your face without your hair getting in the way."

"Why do you want to watch my face?" She'd kind of figured it would be her body he was most interested in.

"When you come, your eyes tilt upward like a cat's and you get this kind of pink glow in your cheeks. It's a turn-on."

So was hearing about it.

She picked up the ribbon, and as she raised her hands to tie back her hair, she felt him watching her, watching her breasts rise and thrust forward with her posture. She took her time, making sure she had a nice ponytail and then tying the ribbon into a pretty bow.

While she was busy tying up her hair, he picked up the body cream and squeezed a dollop into his hand. He started on her breasts, rubbing the cream in large circles that got smaller and smaller as they approached the center. It was warm from the friction, the cream slippy-slidy on her aroused skin. When he palmed her nipples and rubbed she felt like purring.

He rubbed the cream down and over her belly, went back for more and slipped a couple of fingers down between her legs. He rubbed slowly and she moved her hips in time to his rhythm. When he slipped a finger inside her she felt the imminent explosion, felt her legs tremble. "Oh, I'm going to—"

"I know. Look at me."

It was too intimate. She didn't want to, and yet she found herself dropping her gaze to meet his, letting him see what he was doing to her, letting him see inside her to where all the things were hidden that she wasn't ready to say. His eyes stayed steady on hers as he took her up and over, and then finally she slumped to his lap, kissing him, feeling her entire body tremble with reaction.

He was so hard she thought this must be torture for him, and yet he kissed her with more than hunger. She tasted tenderness. Felt it wash over her.

As he went to rise, she stopped him.

"Wait," she panted, and grabbed the sticky pink lip gloss.

He narrowed his eyes at her. "What are you planning to do with that?"

She grinned, uncapped it and painted a thick, sticky pink layer on her lips. She smacked them a few times then she leaned in and kissed his cheek like a grandmother would, leaving a big lip imprint. She moved down to his chest and marked him right over his heart with a big, candy-pink smacker. She slipped off his lap and knelt down, tattooed his belly with her lips, and his lower belly and now he was getting a good idea where she was going, since his erection was bobbing of its own accord, trying to get in on the action. She paused, leaning back on her heels, looking up at him as she uncapped her lip gloss and painted a fresh, thick layer.

"Are you going where I think you're going?"

She smiled, keeping her lips together, and took his cock in her hand. It was hot and hard and beautiful. She kissed the underside first, making a perfect glossy lip print. And another. And another until he looked like he'd been stamped. Then she took him into her mouth.

When they finally ended up in bed, her lip gloss tube was almost empty and they'd both needed another shower.

Holding each other as they settled for sleep, she wondered if maybe he'd told her a truth she'd never believed: the right man would stay. Maybe she'd even found him.

14

MONDAY MORNING on her way into work, Camilla Leeson nearly stumbled when she heard a wolf whistle and realized she was the only woman around. She'd walked past this same construction site dozens of times, and now that she'd had a makeover she was suddenly hot?

Really, she thought, straightening her shoulders a little. Men were so shallow.

When the expensive hairstylist Mercedes had sent her to—after the massage, facial, manicure, pedicure and makeup lesson—started talking to her about adding some gentle highlights, she'd been unsure. How much updating could one person stand in a single day? Mercedes had urged her, "Trust him, he's the best," and so she had.

"We're talking something subtle, a blend of wheat and flax and honey," he had promised, and Camilla thought she would come out looking like a loaf of bread. Instead, her hair looked sophisticated and a little shimmery.

Once her self-indulgence demon had been unleashed, she'd speed tackled her Saturday chores in order to spend an afternoon shopping in Union Square, from the upscale department stores to cozy designer boutiques. The hair and spa pampering had made her feel like a new woman. She had certainly shopped like one. Ignoring the suits, she instead had found herself following a young woman who had a similar multicolored, multilayered hairstyle. And her clothes had smote Camilla with envy. Not hip, exactly, or sexy, exactly, but somehow both.

When a saleswoman had asked if she needed any help, Camilla had abandoned her pride and said, "I want to dress the way that woman does."

Luckily, the saleswoman had understood immediately, and the next two hours—God, she'd shopped for *two* hours—had been the most fun she'd ever had in a store.

Not only had the construction guys noticed her new look, but so had her co-workers, to the point where she almost wished she'd remained dowdy just to avoid all the fuss.

Well, almost.

Around eleven, Mercedes dropped by looking for Dennis. "Hey, you look fantastic," she said the second she saw Camilla. "You bought some new clothes. I'm so glad."

"Thanks." She glanced around. Nobody was listening. Still, she lowered her voice as she told of the amazing development in her made-over life. "The construction guys next door whistled at me."

"No," said Mercedes, trying to sound serious, not quite managing, though. Of course, Mercedes probably needed ear plugs when she went outside of the house, with all the whistling she'd get.

"I know. It sounds pathetic. I'm not the type."

"Sure you are. You just needed some help uncovering your inner sex goddess, that's all."

A quick blush heated her cheeks and she shook her head, getting that wheat field waving.

"Did Dennis notice?"

"I haven't seen him. He's been in court all morning."

"Oh. This is for him. Can you put it on his desk?"

"Sure." Camilla received a brown paper sack, like a lunch bag. It rattled.

"How did the location search go?" Mercedes had refused to talk business on her spa visit, so Camilla was curious to know if her research had helped them find a place.

"Great. This is for you, by the way," she said, handing her a bag that she recognized. This one had the Indulge logo on it.

"You didn't need to—"

"It's a special thanks for booking such nice rooms."

"You're welcome. And?"

Mercedes said, "It's between a great location in Palo Alto and one in Sacramento. The last place was my favorite."

"Isn't it always the way? You could have saved yourself a few days on the road if you'd gone straight there. It's only a couple of hours' drive."

"I didn't mind the nights away." Mercedes's eyes took on the dreamy look of a woman whose business trip had involved a lot of pleasure. She was a gorgeous woman, but the glow on her face and the sparkle in her eyes made her practically incandescent. "We had a fantastic time."

Feeling almost embarrassed to look at a woman so obviously reminiscing about better sex than anything Camilla had even dreamed about, she dropped her gaze to the bag and opened it. "Ohh," she cried, when she recognized the hand and body lotion she'd already decided to splurge on next time she was at Indulge, and a lipstick in the nicest pale copper. She started to say thank you and then was choked by a giggle she hadn't known was there. "You must have had one hell of a trip," she managed between snorts.

"We did." Mercedes took one look at the expensive treats and giggled right along with Camilla.

"Is this a girls-only party or can anybody join in?"

At the sight of Dennis standing behind Mercedes, Camilla tried to stifle her laughter. It was hopeless.

He rolled his gaze, then put a hand on Mercedes's shoulder. It was a casual gesture, though the way he touched her, his fingers curling into her, the way she leaned his way—Camilla bet Mercedes didn't even know she was doing it, as though they were pulled together—declared their intimacy louder than words.

"Did you come to see me?" he asked.

Mercedes glanced up at him, her eyes alight still with the aftermath of laughter and, thought Camilla with a pang of envy, days of fabulous sex. "No. I came to see Camilla. And I brought you something."

Camilla handed him the paper bag. He took it and glanced, puzzled, at Mercedes. "You packed me a lunch?"

A tiny mischievous smile tilted her lips. "No. Just a few things you might need."

He'd been about to open the bag and suddenly stopped, the paper crackling as he rolled it closed. Camilla didn't even want to think about what was in that bag.

"I'll see you later," he said and, not seeming to care who in the office saw him, kissed the startled Mercedes. She put up a slim hand as though she'd stop him. Then, when his lips touched hers, her fingers slid to his shoulder.

As he was about to go to his office, he noticed Camilla for the first time and blinked.

"You look—" His gaze took in her hair, the new clothes, and finally focused on her face as though seeing it was somehow different without understanding why. For which Mercedes and her spa were no doubt responsible. "Wow. You look great."

"Thank you," she said. Coming from Dennis, that was almost as good as a wolf whistle from a construction site.

His secretary told him he was wanted on the phone, and with a what-can-you-do? shrug, he was gone.

"He's right, you know," Mercedes said, with a hint of pride. "You do look great."

"My cat didn't notice, but at least the construction guys and Dennis did. My social life's just booming."

"No husband or boyfriend?" Mercedes asked.

Camilla glanced at her computer as though it were responsible for her single state—which was partly true. "I was too busy with school, then with work." She raised her shoulders in a helpless shrug. "I never was much good at the singles thing. I think every man I've ever dated I met at the library."

"Well," Mercedes said, "at least you knew they liked reading."

"I'm so dull already. I never, ever meet anyone exciting, and that's what I need," she wailed.

"You know what day it is today?"

"Uh, Monday."

"Right." Mercedes stood looking at her for a second, a mysterious expression on her face. "Yes. Monday. Which means that this is your lucky day."

"Wha—"

"Are you busy for lunch?"

"Not really." She'd planned to work through lunch, to help make up for the time she'd missed Friday. Still, she could always stay later and catch up. If Mercedes wanted to have lunch with her, it was well worth staying late after work.

"Good. I'm going to take you to a…secret club."

Her eyes widened. "I thought you were inviting me to lunch."

"I am. Trust me. I'll pick up some sandwiches. Meet me at the spa at 1:00 p.m."

"All right," Camilla said, thinking she wasn't at all sure she liked the idea of a secret club. "Um, I worked my tail off to become a lawyer. I won't end up doing anything I could be disbarred for, will I?"

Even Mercedes's laugh was sexy. "No. I can't tell you more, I have to get to work." And with a wave she was gone.

CAMILLA STEPPED into Indulge at exactly two minutes to one. And then didn't want to leave. It was an oasis of calm, beauty and self-indulgence in the desert of her crazy work life. She stopped to breathe in the wonderful scents and let the atmosphere soak into her skin like one of Mercedes's amazing creams.

Since her makeover, she felt as though she belonged here. She was finally one of the women with the right hair, the right clothes. Her skin was exfoliated, her nails discreetly polished. Even her toes glimmered in a barely-there pink, though no one could see them in her pumps.

She was about to ask for Mercedes, when she saw her. There was something about her that drew the eye. Natural charisma, maybe. Camilla watched her throw a laughing comment over her shoulder to one customer, blow a kiss to another, and then she was there at Camilla's side. "Excellent," she said. "You're right on time. Let's go."

There were two paper sacks in her hand, very much like the one she'd given Dennis. Perhaps she had brought him lunch, after all.

The two women left the spa, and Mercedes said, "Now, I told you this was a sort of secret club and it is. I'm not really supposed to bring anyone who doesn't work in the building." She shrugged, clearly a woman who never met a rule she didn't want to bend. "You come to my spa. Close enough. You can't tell anyone about what you're about to experience, though. You have to promise me."

"Maybe you should give me a hint before we go any further," she said.

Mercedes glanced down the deserted hall. "It's a kind of dating club," she said softly.

"A dating club?"

"Yes. Some single women. We have a sort of dating lottery."

"Lottery?" She imagined a bingo caller yelling out things like, "And under the *B*, a bodybuilder!"

"I can't explain it. You'll have to come and see for yourself. It's in the ladies' lounge."

Camilla was going to a secret dating club? In the bathroom? She wished that she was back at the office immersed in some law text in their library.

Once she'd followed Mercedes into an old-fashioned-style ladies' lounge, she found a group of women eating lunch, giggling and acting like a high-school-cafeteria girls' clique. Exactly the kind of clique from which Camilla had always been excluded. When conversation stopped and all eyes turned to her in surprise, then to Mercedes as if to say, what was *she* doing here? she felt insecurity flood her being that she hadn't experienced in years.

"This is my friend and client, Camilla Leeson. Since I won't be choosing a name today," Mercedes said, with a grin, "Camilla's going to take my turn."

"Do you work in the building?" an Asian woman in a red suit asked.

"No, I—"

"She's a client. She's in my spa all the time." Ha, twice. "She's a lawyer and she's given me a legal oath not to reveal anything that goes on here today. Anybody have a problem?"

"No," said a blond, funky-looking woman with choppy, blond hair. "You absolutely can't tell anyone."

"It's all right." Some imp of mischief made her glance at Mercedes and say, "I've given my legal oath."

"Great. Welcome to the Sisters of the Booty Call. I'm Milla."

"The sisters of the what?"

"Sit down," said Mercedes, passing her a bag. "Eat your sandwich. I'll explain how this works."

It took a few minutes, and since Mercedes got lots of help explaining what the Booty Call club was, Camilla took a while to catch on. Finally, she looked around at the group and said, "So, basically, you pull names of men you've never met, phone them and ask them for a date?"

"You've got it," Milla said.

"Sometimes, we don't do the calling ourselves, if we're very shy," Mercedes said, turning to stare at a sweet-looking woman who stared down at her shoes, not meeting Mercedes's gaze. "Like Rhonda here."

After several seconds of dead silence, Rose spoke up. "I called and set up the date for them."

Milla piped up. "And?"

Finally, the now-blushing Rhonda said, "The dentist was nice. We had lunch."

"And?"

"He said I have a spectacular occlusion."

No one said a word. Finally Milla spoke again. "That's a new one on me."

"I think it means that her teeth are nicely aligned," Camilla offered. It was at times like this that she knew she'd spent way too much of her life in libraries.

"So," Mercedes prompted. "Are you going to see him again?"

"He said he'd call."

"Well, that's wonderful, you got back out there. Good for you."

"Okay," Mercedes said, rising. "If we're all here and

finished eating, I'll handle the boot. I won't be pulling a name today," she said, giving the room the benefit of a smile that conveyed as well as words that she was a well-pleasured woman.

There was a chorus of oohs and a few comments that would have shocked Camilla if she'd let them. These women didn't hold back.

Camilla watched, feeling her eyes grow rounder as each of the women took a business card from the glass boot and made plans, as far as she could tell to phone complete strangers.

In the meantime, the women chatted about grumpy bosses, cramps, bad-hair days, bad dates, a shoe sale, a weight loss. And men, naturally. In that boot were the combined dating detritus of every woman in this room, plus who knew how many former Sisters of the Booty Call.

As the boot drew closer to her, Camilla yearned to be poring over research notes, giving herself eye strain from computer overuse, rather than face that soon it would be her turn.

As, of course, soon it was.

She stared at the boot full of business cards. "I'm not sure I—"

"Pick a card," Mercedes said in a no-nonsense tone.

"Go easy on her," Milla said. "She's a Booty Call virgin."

"Hey," said the pretty young woman, Tamara, who'd been conspicuously silent during the guy-bashing portion of the program, "I know it sounds kind of funky, but the boot does work." Tamara gave her a big smile. "I'm in love." She didn't say another word, simply pointed to the boot.

Camilla was impressed.

"It's true," Rose said, practically reading Camilla's mind. "The boot is good luck. Many matches have been made from there."

She glanced over at Mercedes for confirmation.

"If I hadn't pulled Dennis's card out of there, I wouldn't be walking around with this big smile on my face." Mercedes didn't mention love. Lust however shimmered behind her words.

Camilla really wasn't greedy. If she didn't find the love of her life in a glass cowboy boot, she'd absolutely settle for some great sex. Really, at this point in her dry spell, even some mediocre sex would be perfectly acceptable.

Well, she decided, shoving her hand into the boot, she didn't have to call the guy, whoever he was.

She read the card. So did Mercedes. "Nathan Sherman," the bossy spa owner announced. "Now the back of the card."

Obediently, she turned the card and read a neatly printed message. "Nathan's a sous chef down on the Wharf. He's really good with his hands."

A trill of laughter rippled around the circle of women. "Anybody know the guy?" Mercedes asked.

"No. Uh-uh. Not one of mine."

"I recognize that writing," Mercedes said firmly. "It's Melissa Tong. She moved to L.A. See? Those are her initials, that tiny MT in the corner of the card. If she likes this guy, he's probably a lot of fun. Call him. A chef who's good with his hands. What's not to like?"

"I don't know, I think maybe—"

"Look, honey, it's hard for everybody their first time, right?"

Every woman nodded.

"He wouldn't be in the bowl if he wasn't a decent guy. So, you call him. You talk. Maybe you meet for coffee. Nobody's asking you to marry the guy. Okay?"

"I'm not sure—"

"It's all about trust. You can trust the sisterhood." Since she delivered the last line in a very bad Marlon Brando as the Godfather impersonation, laughter drowned out Camilla's protest, and the boot moved on.

When everybody had a card, and things were obviously winding down, Mercedes rose and Camilla followed suit. "I've got to get back to the spa. See you all next Monday."

"Well, it was great to meet you all," Camilla said. She waved the card in the air. "Thanks for letting me join in."

"Sure, see you next week."

Next week? Surely she wasn't expected—well, she'd tell Mercedes it wasn't her thing, that's all. A dating pool of rejects struck her as a little pathetic. If she was as hard up as that, she could call one of the professional matchmakers in town or join one of those Internet dating sites.

Then she remembered that Dennis McClary had been one of the men in the pool, and she glanced, almost involuntarily at her card. Nathan Sherman. Hmm.

"Come on in to my office," Mercedes said as they passed the spa.

"Oh, no, really. I should get back."

"Unless that law office is a sweat shop, you're allowed more than fifty minutes for lunch. Come on."

They entered by a smaller side door that led to the staff-only area of the spa. Camilla was fascinated by the stacked jars of products, the computer stations, the towels and assorted stuff that went on behind the scenes.

"Do you do your own laundry on-site?" Camilla asked, gazing around her.

"Yes. It's cheaper in the long run than a service, and I'm fussy." Then she fixed her gaze on Camilla. "There's no time for a tour now. We have work to do."

Embarrassed that her delaying ruse had been so transparent, Camilla reluctantly went with Mercedes into a small and very practical-looking office.

She was so surprised, she blinked. "I pictured you in some exotic office with a daybed upholstered in a leopard print, or something."

Her laughter was rich and somehow smoky. "That's good. I want people to have that image of me. It helps my business."

There was a note of pride in the tone, a sort of amazed-that-she-was-pulling-it-off pride that made Camilla say, "This place means everything to you, doesn't it?"

Mercedes paused, and the usual self-possessed, too-gorgeous-to-be-real facade slipped for a second revealing a woman of passion and drive. "Yes. It means a hell of a lot to me."

Then she pointed to the chair behind her desk, moved a rock sitting on the desktop to one side, pulled the phone forward and said, "Call him."

Even though she'd had a pretty good idea Mercedes hadn't dragged her in hear to force a pedicure on her, Camilla still said, "Now?"

"Stop sounding so scared, it'll be fine. I'm going to help you."

"Maybe you could call him for me?"

The brilliant, glossy hair swung as she shook her head. "Uh-uh. This will be good for you."

She picked up the phone, then put down the card and phone. "I don't know what to say."

"You say that Melissa Tong thought you and he might like each other. Then you ask him right out if he's single, in case he hooked up since Melissa tossed the card in the boot. If he is single, then suggest you meet for coffee."

"Coffee? I don't really drink coffee."

"Have a soy-vanilla shake. It doesn't matter. The idea is to meet somewhere open and casual. Feel each other out. See if there's enough compatibility for a date. That's it."

"I'm no good at this."

"You'll get better with practice. Trust me."

"It's lunchtime. He's probably sous-chefing. I should call later."

"You can leave a message if he's not there. Quit stalling!"

Camilla dragged in a breath, thinking how ridiculous this whole thing was, and punched out the number.

The phone rang. Once. Twice. Good, she'd get a machine. And she'd leave a false number. Mercedes would never know and she'd be off the hook.

Liking her idea, she peered up at Mercedes with a reassuring smile, ready for voice mail, when instead, she heard a real, live, though somewhat sleepy and very male voice answer, "Hello?"

She wanted to hang up. If Mercedes hadn't been bending over her like her mother, Dear Abby and Oprah, all rolled into one, she would have.

"Hello?" the voice said again, sharper this time.

"Uh, hello," she said, sounding nervous and ridiculous. Pull yourself together she told herself. "This is Camilla Leeson, from Dunford, Ross and McKay law offices, I was wondering—"

"Am I being sued?"

"No, of course not." Then, because she was unfailingly truthful, she said, "At least, not by me or any of my clients."

He chuckled sleepily. "That's cool. What can I do for you?"

"Um. Well, it's a little personal."

"Do we know each other?"

"No. As far as I know we've never met."

Mercedes tapped a piece of paper, and Camilla saw the name Melissa Tong. "Um, actually, Melissa Tong suggested I call you."

"Huh, no way. How is Melissa?"

No idea. Never met her. "She's fine. She thought… you and I might like each other."

There was a pause. She swallowed noisily. Mercedes was tapping that damn sheet of paper again. *Single?* It said, with several question marks after the word, which had been underscored several times.

"Are you still single?"

"Yeah. Yes, I'm single. Melissa wants to set me up with someone? That's…funny. What did you say your name is again?"

"Camilla Leeson."

Another pause. She could hear the sound of running water and metal banging against metal. He was putting on coffee, she thought. "Did I catch you at a bad time?"

"Sorry, I was napping. I'll be at work until late tonight, so I wanted to grab a few zzzs."

"Oh, I'm sorry."

"No worries."

"Um, would you like to have coffee with me some-time?"

"I don't drink coffee."

She brightened immediately. They already had some-thing in common. "Neither do I," she said before real-izing what a twit that made her sound.

He laughed, a rich, low chuckle that made her suddenly wonder what Melissa Tong had meant when she'd said he had great hands.

"You like milkshakes?"

"Milkshakes? Yes, yes I do."

"Okay. Let's get a milkshake. Tomorrow. I'm free until five."

And Camilla worked until six. On a good day. She had a lunch hour, of course, though going for a milkshake at lunch seemed wrong somehow. Well, she'd figure some-thing out. "How about three o'clock?" she said.

"Perfect. You'll love this place. Real old-fashioned milkshakes."

"Sounds wonderful," she said, thinking that it did.

She scribbled down the address, and the conversation was over. She had no idea how he was going to recognize her, or she him. And he didn't even have her number in case he couldn't make it or something.

She'd done it. She had a sort of date, and it wasn't a hideous foursome of lawyers like the Jerry debacle.

"Congratulations," Mercedes said.

"What if he's an idiot?"

"Then he's an idiot and you'll have had a good milkshake."

15

DENNIS REACHED HIS office and shut the door. He placed the brown paper bag on his desk, regarding it for a moment. Although he had no idea what was in it, his juices were stirring.

He reached forward, opened the bag.

He didn't know what he'd expected. Sex shop goodies, or something wild and silly. Instead, Mercedes had brought him a bag of cherries, fresh from the market. He took one out and munched it. Mmm. Sweet, the flavor burst in his mouth. A little the way Mercedes did when he…

What was she dropping off cherries for? He was mildly disappointed, even slightly pissed that she was leading him on with an intriguing bag, getting his hopes up, for…a bag of fruit?

Nice fruit, though. Sweet. He reached into the paper sack for another cherry and his finger bumped into something that definitely wasn't a cherry. Wondering why he'd doubted her for a second, and somehow relieved that she had more in mind than him getting his five fruits and veg a day, he dug down to find a candle and matches. A bar of Ghirardelli chocolate, and one of those free makeover cards to her salon that she loved to hand out.

There was a note clipped to it. "Dear Dennis. Thanks for all your help on the road trip. Come by the spa tonight, around eight. I'd like to thank you with my unique spa special, for you alone. The full treatment."

He was grinning like a fool when he got to the end of the note, where a p.s. was scribbled. "Bring the contents of the bag. Don't eat all the cherries."

Her spa closed at six on Monday nights. By eight, there'd be no one around except him and Mercedes. He'd never had any interest in going to a spa in his life. Now, here he was going twice in less than two weeks? Still, he reminded himself, Mercedes's full treatment for him alone was likely to be a little different from the very nice, though impersonal, massage he'd enjoyed in the resort spa.

He could barely concentrate on work, which was not like him. Every time he saw that bag his groin tightened as though Mercedes had reached down and taken him in hand.

Camilla came in twice and he saw her look at the bag with mild curiosity. Her makeover seemed to have affected her. She seemed a bit flustered and he could have sworn that her mind was somewhere else.

A problem he could relate to. He had no idea what Mercedes had planned for that candle or the cherries. He was a creative guy and was having no trouble coming up with all kinds of ideas.

Finally, when he'd let his attention wander once too often, he took the bag, shoved it in his briefcase and locked the thing.

He would have taken a midday break at the gym to try and work off some steam except that he had a lunch with a client. At lunch he made sure to eat lots of protein. He'd be needing his strength later, he figured.

DENNIS FELT a little foolish walking into an almost empty office building at eight o'clock at night holding a brown paper lunch bag. Luckily there was nobody there other than the night security guard who'd been told to expect Dennis.

His body was so ready for action he felt his cock leading the way like an arrow. When he got to the door of Indulge, he didn't think he'd ever been as horny in his life. He entered the spa and found it in darkness.

"Mercedes?" he called softly. He could hear tiny sounds coming from somewhere, yet she didn't answer him. He reached behind him to feel around for a light switch, when he remembered the candle in his bag.

"You are one crazy woman, you know that?" he said, rooting around for the matches and candle. He somehow got the candle lit without dropping the bag, and the smell of burned match soon melded with the scent of beeswax. The candle glowed a deep gold and there was a line of identical candles creating a path ahead of him.

Pausing only to lock the front door of the spa, he bent and, using his one burning candle, lit them all. The atmosphere of Indulge was always sensual and smelled, felt, damn near tasted, like a hedonistic retreat. The candlelight added romance to the mix.

The burning path he lit led him to a closed door. He knocked.

"Come in," she said.

He opened the door and very nearly dropped the candle. Mercedes was wearing a see-through button-up blouse that hung to her thighs, a pair of beaded flip-flops and not another thing.

"You can light the rest of the candles," she said to him, in the same professional tone his dental hygienist used when she asked him to spit.

He, who used words to argue cases, win lawsuits and charm clients, was struck dumb.

He saw more candles and lit them all. He realized that he'd never been inside one of her treatment rooms until now. There was a narrow bed made up with crisp linens, a machine was making a burbling sound and sending a sharpish scent that might have been pine or cedar into the air. A cart of creams and things sat behind him.

"Please remove all your clothes and get onto the bed," she said in that same professional voice.

"All of them?"

She flicked him a glance. "Yes."

Then she walked out. Like she was his chiropractor and he needed privacy.

He doubted she'd ever had a client get themselves naked and under that white sheet so fast, or one who bellowed, "Ready!"

She made him wait at least three minutes. Somehow, he'd known she would. Then she knocked softly before entering. Maybe she was acting like a professional aesthetician. Still, the way her nipples thrust against the sheer silky fabric like gold nuggets, told him her excitement level was as high as his.

"Have you ever had a facial before?" she asked.

"A facial?" He raised up to his elbows and stared at her. "Are you trying to kill me?"

Her lips twitched but she said, "It's step one of the full treatment."

Well, he might be a sucker for Mercedes but he wasn't stupid. "What's step two?"

She wasn't stupid, either. She merely tilted her lips in a knowing smile. "It's a surprise."

In Dennis's mind, the only thing that made the facial worthwhile was the sight of Mercedes's breasts taunting him as she worked. She spread some kind of goop onto his face, his nose and forehead, even his neck. Thankfully it didn't smell like girly stuff. It was more of the man-of-the-woods scent he'd noticed when he walked in. And, damn it, the stuff felt great. She had wonderful hands and strong fingers, and when she got to massaging his shoulders, he began to think maybe sex wasn't the only thing worth coming for tonight.

When she'd removed the gunk with some other, lighter cream, he began to feel that holding on to an erection this long couldn't be good for a guy. He motioned to the bag he'd put on the counter when he undressed. "What about the cherries?"

"I haven't forgotten them."

The touch of her fingers as she wiped and pressed and kneaded was so good he half forgot the raging need roaring through him.

He'd have closed his eyes except he didn't want to miss the view.

"Have you ever had a sea-salt body scrub?" she asked him.

He gave her the best impression of a take-no-prison-ers gunfighter a man could give who was naked in a spa at the tail end of a facial. "If we don't move onto the you-and-me-doing-the-nasty portion of the evening, I'm going to have you flat on your back on this table in about five seconds, and I'll be the one giving you the full treatment."

For a second her nostrils flared and he thought he might taste her temper, then her mood changed as quickly again and she laughed. "You have no willpower at all, do you?"

"Not where you're concerned."

She shook her head. "The full treatment usually involves a sea-salt body scrub. I can see you're not in the right—" she looked at his crotch where he'd made a tent of the white sheet "—frame of mind."

She rustled in the bag, took out the chocolate. He watched her, hearing the tear of the wrapper, the crinkle of silver paper. The chocolate was smooth, dark and, in her hands, sensual.

"We'll move onto something I think you're ready for."

She flipped back the sheet, revealing his naked and eager body.

She picked up one of the candles, and then held the chocolate to the flame. Over his naked chest. "You have to be careful," she said, "or the chocolate burns."

This didn't burn; it dripped, long, dark ribbons of chocolate. It was warm when it hit his chest, yet not un-pleasantly so. She was careful with the candle, turning it so the wax never dripped on him, only the chocolate. "I love chocolate," she said.

She took a cherry, swirled it in the melted bar and then held it to his mouth. He bit, avoiding the pit. She put the other half in her mouth, then popped the pit into her hand and threw it in the wastebasket in the corner. The cherry was so sweet, the chocolate rich and dark.

She took another cherry, dipped that in the melting chocolate and, instead of putting it in his mouth, as he'd half expected, she used it like a paintbrush. Holding the stem and dragging the cherry with the still-wet chocolate down his belly. Since he had a hopeful idea of where this was going, he held his breath, feeling the warmth on his skin. His muscles tightened, jerked as she left a trail of sweetness. His cock was throbbing, fit to burst, and she must have known it. She did the cherry-into-chocolate routine again, and he was so desperate he heard himself groan as the cherry moved toward his groin. She smiled a little and finally touched the coated fruit to his aching flesh. If anything, it was greater torture than the waiting. The motion was too soft to bring relief, too insistent to be ignored.

Up and down the shaft she painted him, obviously enjoying herself.

It took all his willpower not to drag that silly wisp of cloud she called a shirt up and take her, chocolate and all. He was determined to show her he could wait. If it killed him.

This was her show, and he had a very good feeling, knowing Mercedes, that the reward would be worth the wait.

"I love the way you look in chocolate," she said, as if she were his personal stylist. "It's a good look for you."

"I love how you look in the candlelight and that shirt," he rasped, sneaking his hand out and slipping it under the hem to caress her ass.

"Oh, that's nice," she murmured. Then she bent over and touched her tongue to him. He'd imagined she'd lick the chocolate off his body in the same order she'd applied it; he pretty much figured that had been her plan, too. Either she was trying to surprise him, once again, or she was as impatient as he. She licked her way up his shaft, slowly, and he was sure he could feel the chocolate melting between her tongue and his skin, he felt her glide and swirl over him, tease him, only a little, then take him very slowly, very deliberately, out of his mind.

He thought that he would never again smell any kind of tree, or even see a bar of chocolate, without being reminded of this moment.

When he opened his eyes, she was chewing a cherry, with a rather pleased expression on her face. She'd blown his mind and she knew it.

"Now," she said, back to her dental hygienist efficiency, "the next step is our eucalyptus steam room. Very popular with men."

He held up a hand. "I don't think we're finished in here," he said.

"Well…"

"There's more chocolate," he reminded her. "And more cherries."

She was so hot he could scent her arousal, as a sharp

and exotic undertone to the pine, cedar or whatever it was, and the chocolate.

"What do you have in mind?"

"Why don't you change places with me and find out?"

Her eyes blazed suddenly and his oh, so satisfied cock stirred. He wondered if they'd ever quench this heat that burned between them. The lust was so strong he sometimes thought they'd both almost missed the less-fiery-but-forever love that he now recognized was between them.

He was off that bed fast, before she changed her mind, saying, "I love this top, I don't want to mess it up." He slid the buttons open, peeled the whisper of nothing off her skin and then couldn't resist putting his mouth to the center of her chest. She smelled, felt, tasted so good. A hint of salt, a touch of something sweet and homey, vanilla maybe or honey. Because he wanted to, he bent and lifted her high, startling a laugh out of her. Then he placed her on the bed.

"I bet you've never had a treatment here before."

"Well, the new hires all practice on me before I let them touch clients."

He smiled. "You're going to like what I do to you better."

"Egotist," she said. She couldn't prevent the little smile that played over her mouth, though, any more than he could help himself kissing her.

Then he got to work.

There was about half the bar of chocolate left. He wasn't going to fool around with candle wax, didn't figure he had her dexterity, and the last thing he wanted was to burn her. He figured her skin was hot enough.

First, he rustled around in the bag for a cherry. He pulled out a handful, choosing a good, fat one. He glanced at Mercedes and saw her watching him through half-closed eyes. The candlelight turned her skin to gold. His breath caught for a moment and time seemed to still. Then a flame flickered and he pulled himself back to the moment.

He stepped to the bed, touched the cherry between her breasts and dragged it slowly down the centre of her body. She sighed out a breath, and he could have sworn it trembled. He paused when he got to her belly button, and her eyes widened. Was he going to leave it there?

No. He was not.

16

MERCEDES FELT the trembling inside her, under her skin. The fruit was firm, silky and warming as it trailed across her body.

Dennis had an intent expression on his face, as though he was memorizing her.

She felt the fruit moving over her belly, the soft brush as it moved through her curls. He wouldn't...

"Spread your legs," he said softly.

A tiny sound, half gasp, half sigh escaped. Still she did as he asked. She was so hot, so restless, so desperate. She'd forgotten when she planned her little spa experience for one that she'd end up as riled as Dennis.

She opened for him. Not coyly, but all the way, letting the soles of her feet meet so she was bowed open.

"Thank you," he said, so softly.

He bent over her, and she felt his fingers on her, felt her own need begin to overpower her. He pushed the cherry into her. Not all the way, just enough to open her, and hold her there.

Her hips jerked helplessly, and he glanced down at her, so obviously enjoying his power over her, as she'd enjoyed hers over him.

Then he picked up the chocolate bar. He didn't reach for the candle though, which was just as well, she thought. Instead he took the still-soft end and rubbed it over her breast. It scraped softly, bumped the nub of her nipple, and then she felt the softening as the chocolate warmed against her skin. It was gooey and thick, smearing over her breasts as Dennis rubbed it with all the glee of a little kid in a mud puddle.

She giggled, feeling ridiculous, foolish and so hot that any second she was going to blow that cherry like a champagne cork.

He took his mouth to her breasts, licking chocolate off her, smearing it; rough stubble and soft tongue and firm lips all driving her wild until she was rolling and giggling and panting all at once.

"Please," she moaned at last, and he stopped teasing, trailing his tongue along the same path the cherry had taken.

When he reached the cherry, he traced it with his tongue, making her arch her back. He tracked up a little to her hot button, tonguing her until she was sobbing, her legs trembling and her hips bucking.

The pressure built inside her until she couldn't take any more, and with a great whoosh, she felt the wave of pleasure roll through her. Her head was thrown back, her hips right up off the bed, and then he took her hips in his hands. And sucked the cherry out of her and into his mouth.

He walked up to the top of the bed, chewing. Unable to speak, she wrapped her arms around his hips and leaned her head against his belly.

"I took your cherry," he teased.

She laughed weakly. "You've been holding on to that line all day, haven't you."

Even though the bed was too small for two, he hiked up and joined her there. She didn't argue or resist, merely watched him with those eyes as dark and rich as anything a chocolatier had dreamed up.

She was still open to him, her body still pulsing with pleasure. He knew her so well, knew she'd only begun. The short break had been enough for him. He was ready for more. He entered her slowly, watching her face in the flickering light of the candles. There was a tiny smear of chocolate on her lower lip. When he kissed her, he tasted chocolate and cherry. And her.

They were in such perfect harmony as they moved that when they climaxed together, it seemed absolutely natural. He flipped them, so she was nestled on top of him and his arms were wrapped around her.

Their hearts beat in unison, as though something momentous had happened. For a long moment they lay there, and he felt them both resist leaving that perfect place where they were more one person than two. Then her face altered subtly, and he felt her mask slip back into place. He couldn't bear it.

"Come on, lover. We've both got to work tomorrow." Her tone was casual, but he wasn't fooled.

"Mercedes," he whispered, his body replete, his mind so full of love for her he couldn't hold it in any longer. "I love you."

He didn't know what he'd expected she'd do when he said those words. Cry? Hug him? Start planning the wedding? Whisper them back?

He got none of those reactions. She stiffened, her whole body suddenly clenching, and then she relaxed, deliberately it seemed to him, and she laughed softly. "No, you don't."

"Yeah, I do."

"What we have is hot, amazing. It's sex. Uncomplicated, fabulous, mutually enjoyable sex." She kissed his nose. "Don't make more of it than it is."

He could not believe what he was hearing. Okay, his feelings were hurt big-time, he acknowledged that. She was trying to turn something amazing into a garden-variety affair. Why would she do that?

Under his hurt and, yes, he admitted, his anger, there was a feeling he couldn't grasp. Mercedes wasn't uninvolved, he knew that as well as he knew the sound of her voice when she cried out his name in climax, as well as he knew the feel of her body, going crazy beneath him, above him, around him.

Maybe she didn't love him; he was no expert. He'd only ever had this happen to him once in his life, yet he was pretty damn sure all that love wasn't coming from him alone.

He'd given her enough hints of his feelings when they were on the road, and he'd given her time to get used to the idea of his love. Of him being part of her future.

And then it hit him. "You're scared."

She groaned and wiggled away from him, off the bed. "I'm getting cold," she said, and rolled away and started pulling on her clothes.

"Cold feet?"

"Cold everything." She had her street clothes in a

basket at the bottom of the trolley and he watched, stunned, as she wriggled into her panties, pulled her shirt over her head and then looked at him. "We're having such a great time. Please don't spoil it."

He blinked. Feeling odd and very, very foolish. "Me loving you would spoil this?" He heard the pain in his own voice and was even more furious. "I don't believe it."

She glanced at him, the smooth, gorgeous mask well in place. "Come on. We still have time for that eucalyptus steam room if you want."

"I think I'm done with the full treatment, thanks."

"Hey," her hand on his arm was soft, though in his anger it felt like a claw. "I never said I wanted more."

He rose and started to shove himself into his clothes. "My mistake."

CAMILLA HAD DONE HER BEST not to dress too much like a lawyer. Still she didn't look like the kind of woman who'd stop in for a milkshake at three in the afternoon, either. She wore black slacks, low slung and tighter than anything she'd ever worn before to the office, and a gray and silver top with words printed on it. They were Latin, presumably meant to be incomprehensible, but Camilla had aced Latin and knew she had scraps of the *Iliad* on her chest. She loved words. So wearing them gave her added confidence, plus the *Iliad* was a story of a quest. How appropriate.

She'd redone her makeup at lunch, and her hair was still cooperating. She'd never be Cameron Diaz, but she knew she looked her best. She found the milkshake place, which was really an old-fashioned-style diner, near the wharf.

She parked and dragged off the long jacket that had successfully hidden how tight her pants were and the mild sexiness of the top. She grabbed her bag, sucked in one more breath hoping for confidence and walked across the street to the diner. She was always early. She couldn't help it. Punctuality was as much a part of her nature as honesty. Naturally, she'd be first here, so she'd brought some work.

She entered the diner and for a second forgot her nerves. It was like something out of the fifties. Red vinyl booths, real soda glasses, a juke box. She hadn't been a child of the fifties, of course. She hadn't been born until the seventies, but this place made her feel as nostalgic as though she'd personally screamed when Elvis had performed on *The Ed Sullivan Show.*

She scanned the customers, mostly families or couples, not many singles. Luckily there were enough vacant booths that she could wait—or be stood up— without it being a huge issue. She noticed a guy sitting alone at a booth, reading a book. He glanced up at her and gave her a quizzical look, then checked his watch.

Couldn't be. He was young. Maybe a year or two younger than her. Longish hair, a narrow face and eyes of a brilliant green.

"Camilla?" he said the word softly, so mostly she saw the movement of his lips and guessed he was saying her name.

She nodded and walked over to him.

"You're early," he said.

"Always," she admitted.

He grinned. "Me, too."

"And we both hate coffee."

He grinned and she thought it was one of the sexiest sights she'd ever seen. "Let's just get married and save ourselves a bunch of time."

She laughed. She'd been so nervous and felt such a fool, and here he was, earlier than she and already making her feel at ease.

She held out her hand. "Camilla Leeson."

The grin, which hadn't even faded yet, intensified. "Nathan Sherman."

Their hands met, and she glanced at his, thinking again of that odd note Melissa Tong had so carefully printed on the back of his business card. He had long fingers, quite slim for a man, and beautiful, except for several scars. From handling sharp knives, she imagined.

For a second she imagined those wonderful, strong, scarred hands on her own skin and was shocked. Had it been that long?

Yes, she realized.

It had.

She settled into the booth, across from him.

"So," he said, "what's your flavor?"

"Chocolate," she said. "I know it's boring—"

"There is no other kind of milkshake."

She sighed, thinking that was three things they already agreed on. "Exactly."

He was gone before she could say or do anything. And soon returned with two huge milkshakes in tall, authentic milkshake glasses.

"This was a great idea," she said, taking a long pull through the straw, the shake so thick that she felt her cheeks cave in.

"Well?" he asked, when she'd licked her lips after that first incredible taste, waiting for her response as though he'd personally made the shakes and her opinion was important.

"Much better than coffee." Then she giggled. "This is like something out of a *Happy Days* rerun."

Then she could have bitten her tongue off. How pathetic to admit she watched reruns of old sitcoms.

He chuckled. "You can just imagine Richie and Fonzie in the next booth, can't you?"

"You watch *Happy Days,* too?"

He shrugged. "I work nights. *Happy Days, Get Smart,* game shows and soaps is what I watch."

"No cooking shows?"

He glanced up at her over his straw. "Do you watch *Boston Legal* in your spare time?"

"Ah," she said, nodding. "Got you."

"So, when you're not suing people, what do you do?"

"Actually, I'm a research lawyer. I don't sue anyone. I gather all the facts, find precedents, that sort of thing."

"Do you like it?" he asked with the same sort of fascination he might ask someone who ate bugs how they tasted.

"I'm very good at what I do, and yes, most of the time I do enjoy my work."

"Huh. Different strokes."

"How about you? How did you get into cooking?"

"I took over the cooking at home when I was twelve, and it was clear to everybody that I was a way better cook than my mom."

"Ouch. Did that cause problems?"

"Nope. My mom's a doctor. Not exactly home a lot. We didn't want to have a housekeeper anymore so my sister and I made a deal with her. It worked out okay."

She nodded, liking his openness.

"I bought cookbooks the way other guys bought *Hustler.*"

"Your mom must be so proud."

He took his straw and made a little pattern in the top of his shake. "She wants me to open my own restaurant. She's offered to back me, but…"

"You want your independence?" she guessed.

"Nothing so noble. I don't want my own restaurant. I don't want the responsibility and worrying at three in the morning that I won't be able to cover payroll this month. All I want to do is cook. Learn. Get better. You know?"

"I think so."

They sat over empty milkshake glasses and talked about everything. Childhoods, jobs, friends, families, hobbies. Not that Camilla had many hobbies. Work was taking up too much of her life. She loved hearing Nathan talk about surfing and trolling flea markets and junk shops for old cooking gadgets, and the weekly Scrabble game he played with three women at a vegan café. She told herself that if he was interested in one or all three of the women, he wouldn't have brought up the weekly game, then told herself she shouldn't care so much about a man she'd just met, then worried that she did like him and maybe she was being too eager.

Suddenly he glanced up at the big round stainless steel clock on the wall and cursed. "I gotta go. I'm late."

"Oh, I'm so sorry. I've kept you talking too long."

"I had a great time," he said, rising. "So, do you want to take a chance on an actual date?"

She'd been ready for him to breeze out of her life as easily as he'd breezed in. At his words she nodded, too eagerly, probably, as his easy smile dawned once more.

"Here's my number," she said, pulling out a business card and scribbling her home number on it.

He took the card and stuffed it in his pocket. "Great, I'll call you." He stared at her for a moment, and she thought for a mad second he was going to kiss her, then he gave her shoulder a squeeze and was gone.

CAMILLA TRIED not to think about Nathan. It was too incredible that somebody she hadn't met in a library or at school or a law function might seriously want to date her.

It was the makeover, she was sure. She was advertising herself as something she wasn't, and that, she worried deeply, could only cause trouble.

Then Nathan called her at home that night and she forgot she was more about brains than beauty, efficiency than sexuality. The warm charm in his voice rolled over her making her feel both beautiful and sexy.

"I had a good time yesterday," he said.

In the background she heard clanging and voices, the whirr of some kind of machinery. Somebody yelled something in French.

"Me, too. Thanks for the milkshake."

"Listen, I'm at work so I can't talk too long. I was wondering about the weekend? Do you want to get together Saturday morning? I don't have to be at work until four."

"All right. Sure. I'd love to." Too late she realized that

she should at least have pretended she needed to check her schedule.

He didn't seem to notice her pathetic lack of conflict, though. "That's great. Why don't you meet me at ten at the intersection of Grant and Bush."

"Chinatown?"

"Sure. We'll hang out. Go for dim sum."

"Okay."

And so she did. She even bought new jeans for the occasion, though she seemed to have paid a lot extra for them to look as though they'd been worn by generations of women, washed a hundred times, beaten, slashed and stomped on.

Nathan was waiting for her, his hands in his pockets. His eyes narrowed when he smiled, which he did when he saw her.

They walked Chinatown, and ate dim sum and she bought a paper lantern for her apartment and he bought some kind of sesame oil. He was such easy company that she found herself forgetting she was no good with men. Until he suddenly lifted his hand to her cheek, leaned in slowly and kissed her.

She was so surprised she lost her balance and grabbed at his shoulders, which he misunderstood for roaring passion she presumed, since he followed her stumbling self until she was pressed against the faded brick of an old building, and he was pressed against her front, still kissing her. But deeper, the kind of kiss that said, I want to have sex with you.

He pulled away after a long time and looked down at her face. He pushed a stray strand of wheat, barley or corn off her cheek and tucked it behind her ear. "I want to cook for you," he said.

"Oh." So, she'd thought he wanted to have sex. Of course she was wrong. She misunderstood sex signals all the time.

"Tomorrow's my night off. Why don't you come to my place and I'll cook?"

"Tomorrow's Sunday. Isn't your restaurant open?"

His eyes gleamed green and wicked. "I've got the brunch shift. That gives me the whole night off."

"Oh," she said again, stupidly. Okay, only a moron would miss that, if he was talking the whole night, he had more than risotto in mind.

WHEN MERCEDES SAW the e-mail header, "Help!!," she first thought it was spam. She clicked open the message when she saw Camilla's name.

I have to talk to you. Help me. Dating disaster.

Mercedes was busy. It was Saturday, nonetheless she felt a certain Pygmalian pride in Camilla. She'd helped get that dry skin dewy, steered her to hair, makeup and clothes that made the poor woman look her age and brought out her best features. And she'd made her take the plunge into the world of men.

The word *disaster* did not make her feel comfortable. She contemplated e-mailing back, then picked up the phone. It was answered at once.

"Hey, Camilla, it's Mercedes. What's up?"

"I don't know what to do."

"How was your date with the sous chef?" Mercedes asked, feeling alarmed. The whole point of the boot was to preselect guys. Surely Camilla hadn't hooked a shark or a dogfish on her first fishing expedition?

"It was wonderful." The practical voice on the other end was suddenly breathless and soft.

"So, what's the problem? Wonderful doesn't sound like a disaster."

"Tomorrow will be."

"Why?"

"He's cooking me dinner. The way things are going, I'm thinking he, I'm worried we'll—"

"Have sex?"

"Yes."

"Honey, if you're not ready, just say no."

"I am ready. I think. It's just that I'm no good at...at any of it."

There was a suggestion of panic in the tone, so she said, "Okay, do you want to get together and talk about it?"

"No. I can't talk about this face-to-face. It's too embarrassing."

"The phone's fine," Mercedes said soothingly, checking her watch. She had ten minutes. Not enough time to do much, so she was going to have to go with big-picture stuff.

"What specifically are you no good at?"

"Sex!"

From what Mercedes had been able to guess about Camilla, she pegged her for an overachiever. "Is it possible you're being too hard on yourself?"

"No."

"Okay. Maybe it's not you. Maybe you've had, um, unsatisfactory partners."

"I don't know. I've only slept with three men, and I met them all at the library."

"Really?"

"Yes. And the thing is, when I got to having sex I was usually thinking about case law and got distracted."

Glad they were doing this by phone so Camilla couldn't see her smile, she said, "That definitely sounds like the wrong partner."

"Well," Camilla admitted, "I always got the feeling they were thinking about something else, too."

"You want advice?"

"No. Mostly I want to tell you that this whole thing was a stupid idea. The thing is, I look like somebody I'm not. He's going to expect a woman who is, well, hip and exciting."

"Honey, you've spent two long dates together. Maybe he likes you. Not your hair or your dewy skin, but you."

"I can't do it. Sex ruins everything."

"Well, there is no law that says you have to sleep with a man on the third date, you know. Tell him it's too soon."

"And if I decide to go ahead?"

A small grin of satisfaction curled Mercedes's lips. "Relax. Think about him. Touch his hair, touch his skin. Tell him what feels good. Ask him what he likes."

"Ask him?"

"Sure. Everybody is different. If you ask him what he likes, it's going to be a lot easier for him to ask you the same question. And a guy who doesn't want to learn your body isn't worth your time."

"I don't know…"

"Well, if you're not ready, you're not. If you decide you are, then relax and let go."

"Easy for you to say."

"Oh, and Camilla?"

"Yes?"

"No case law in the bedroom. Got it?"

A soft chuckle answered her. "Thanks." There was a pause, then Camilla said, "Is everything okay with you and Dennis?"

Apart from the fact that they hadn't seen each other since Monday? And she didn't know what to do about the whole I-love-you thing? "Why do you ask?"

"Well, it's none of my business if you don't want to talk about it. Dennis has been a raging bear all week. I thought maybe you had a fight or something."

Mercedes blew out a breath, wishing she could blow out her unhappiness with it. "It's complicated." And surprisingly she was dying to unburden herself. Hell, if Camilla could talk about fear of sex, surely she could open up about her own fears.

"He said he loves me."

"Wow," Camilla breathed. "And why is that not a good thing?"

"If I could figure that out, maybe Dennis and I could talk about this and he wouldn't be so much of a raging bear and I wouldn't feel like I had terminal PMS."

"I'm so sorry. I wish I could be as helpful as you've been. All I know is that you both looked so happy together."

The words had a lump forming in Mercedes's throat,

and she sure didn't have time for that. "I'm sure I'll work it out. Good luck with the date tomorrow. Tell me all about it on Monday, okay?" she said, hoping that she sounded upbeat when she was suddenly feeling anything but.

17

"YOU DON'T LIKE THE SCALLOPS?" Nathan looked at her with concern.

"Yes. I do. Everything's delicious."

"Then how come you're pushing your food around your plate? Hiding a scallop under a lettuce leaf does not fool me."

She watched him eating, his hands, those beautiful, battle-scarred, sensitive hands that had prepared her food. She imagined them touching her skin and dropped her fork. "I'm too nervous to eat," she admitted miserably.

"Why?"

She waved her hands around her head as though a bee were after her. "It's the whole sex thing. It's freaking me out."

He blinked in surprise. "What sex thing?"

She flapped a hand between them. "This. The two of us alone. Tonight. Will we? Won't we? What if it's terrible? I can't stand it."

She thought a tiny gleam of humor lit his eyes, but it was gone so fast she could have imagined it. He poured more wine, and she thought the heavy silence would be the death of her. She'd keel over dead and the coroner's report would simply read, "Camilla Leeson. Twenty-six. Time of death, 21:20. Died of embarrassment."

"So, we won't," he said, calm and reasonable.

She stared at him. "We won't?"

"No. We'll decide right now that we won't have sex tonight." He replaced the wine bottle on the table and picked up his knife and fork. "And you'll eat."

"I can't tell you what a relief that is," she said with a sigh, finally biting into a scallop and tasting it.

She was swallowing the scallop when she realized what she'd implied. She looked up and found him smiling at her.

"There's just nothing I can say to make that any better, is there?"

"My advice? Don't even try."

And somehow it was okay. Without the stupid sex thing hanging over her, she actually tasted the food he'd cooked and caught herself moaning with pleasure. "This is fantastic."

"Thanks. I thought we'd have dessert up on the roof."

"You're kidding me."

"No. There's a roof patio. Great view. It's the best part about this apartment."

Dessert was a lemony, frothy mouthwatering delight that he'd put in soda glasses. She laughed, thinking of the milkshakes they'd met over. It felt like she'd known him a lot longer than a week.

The night sky was clear enough that you could see a few stars, lights twinkling over the bay. There were a couple of battered loungers on the roof patio and a round metal table with a hole in it for an umbrella that had seen better days. They sat in two plastic Adirondack chairs and ate their desserts with long spoons that were a little dented. "Did you get these at a restaurant?"

"No. I told you I go to antique stores and junk shops. I like buying old kitchen stuff. It's my hobby. Which is how I have vintage food appliances and plates and cutlery and stuff."

Now she thought about it, they'd eaten with fish knives and forks with mother-of-pearl handles. And soft green Depression-glass plates. She'd assumed they were family hand-me-downs.

Up here on the roof she felt so far from her everyday world, almost as though she could reach out with her long-handled spoon and scoop a star. A long sigh of contentment rolled through her.

After finishing her dessert, she put the glass down on the floor beside her. "When I look out at the harbor," she said, "I always want to get on a boat and go somewhere. Sail away."

"Where?"

"Oh, it's only a silly dream."

"Where does your boat sail in your silly dream?"

"The Greek Islands."

"Good choice. You ever been?"

"To Greece? No. I've never been off this continent."

"The islands are fantastic. You've never seen water so blue. I spent a few months there."

"I envy you."

"It was a working cruise. One good thing about cooking is it's always easy to find a job. I crewed for a sailing charter. Saw a lot of places."

"Next to you I feel so dull."

"Hey, don't be hard on yourself. I could never study long enough to become a lawyer. Come to think of it, my grades probably weren't good enough, anyway."

She glanced over to say something to him and found he'd risen and was crouching before her. Something about the expression in his eyes made her heart pound. "I think that you are beautiful, and smart, and sexy," he said.

"You do?"

He didn't answer. Instead he ran his hands up her thighs, raising himself up enough to kiss her. And kaboom. Rockets went off. He tasted like cool lemon and hot male. His hair brushed her cheek when he changed the angle of the kiss. Her hands gripped his shoulders, kneading, rubbing, up into his hair, which was surprisingly soft.

He kissed her as though his whole purpose in life was to kiss. His hands touched her gently, feathering over her hair, down her arms, across her chest making her shiver and want more.

She didn't even notice he'd snuck under her shirt until she felt his fingers on her stomach, so light and sure. A little higher, over her ribs, and then he was tracing the lacy cups of her bra, toying with her breasts. Oh, how good it felt. How wonderful and thrilling.

He traced her bra to the back clasp and she leaned forward so he could release her. The touch of his fingers changed, a little firmer, more insistent. She felt the brush of fabric on her belly, then dimly realized he was raising her top up, over her breasts, so she felt the cool night air tingle across her nipples.

When he put his mouth there, she moaned helplessly.

"You taste so good," he said.

"It's this body lotion I get at Indulge." She gasped as he sucked lightly. "It's a spa."

He trailed his tongue around and around. "I wonder what herbs they're using. This stuff is great. I could cook with these herbs."

She wanted to see him, feel him, so she took the bold step of pulling his polo shirt off. He was wiry, on the thin side, but muscular. He had a tiny tattoo of an anchor on his chest. For some reason, the sight of it filled her with unaccustomed lust.

She pictured him on that ship in the Greek Islands. His hair would be sun kissed, his body brown. He'd taste like salt and olives and lemons. Her mouth watered, wanting him.

There was a bulge at her eye level and she shocked herself when she found herself cupping him, rubbing the beautiful, hot length of him through his jeans.

"We should go downstairs," he said, panting a little.

She yanked her hand back as though she'd burned it. "Oh, what am I thinking?" All her stupid fears and foolishness rushed back. She jumped to her feet, fumbling her top back down, leaving her bra unfastened. "I've got to get home. I've got work tomorrow."

For a second he looked at her, his disappointment keen. "Okay." Picking up his shirt, he didn't bother to put it back on, as he gathered up the empty dessert dishes before following her downstairs.

Back in his apartment she refastened her bra, ran a hand through her hair. "Can I help you with the dishes?" she said, feeling utterly foolish.

"No. It's okay. I got it."

She pushed a hand through her hair, realized she'd just done that two seconds ago and dropped her hand to her side. "Thanks for dinner. It was wonderful."

"You're welcome."

She found her purse, hooked it over her shoulder.

"I'll call you," he said. And kissed her softly.

"Good night," she said, heading for the door.

"Hey."

She'd reached the door. She halted, too embarrassed to turn.

"Want to grab lunch Wednesday?"

Only now did it hit her that she'd assumed she wouldn't see him again.

She kept her gaze on the door. "Wednesday? I think I can do Wednesday. I'll let you know."

"Great."

The door was open. She took a step out.

Then she spun around. It was as if her feet had a different agenda from the rest of her. He was standing, his jeans slung low on his hips, the anchor weighing on that muscled torso, arms crossed, one shoulder leaning against the wall. She moved forward, faster, noted his lean face: those penetrating green eyes that could see her, all of her; the unruly hair; the mouth that made her weak at the knees when he kissed her, licked her nipples and when he talked to her.

Walk away from this?

Only a fool would do that.

She went all the way up to him. He didn't move. Not a muscle, though his gaze never left hers.

She threw an arm around his neck, pulled his head down, kissed him, her mouth open and hungry.

Now his arms came around her and they stood there, against the opening to the galley kitchen, kissing.

Somehow she knew that the big move had to be hers.

She didn't say a word as she led him to the bedroom and kicked the door shut behind her.

She kept moving forward until they hit the bed. He fell back, pulling her with him so she landed on top of him.

"You sure about this?"

She took his hand and placed it on her breast. "Shut up."

He didn't have to be told twice. Those clever, amazing hands soon had her stripped naked and then they moved, on her, in her, taking her to climax before she'd really thought about it. Before she'd thought about anything. In fact, thought had nothing to do with what was going on in that bedroom. It was all about feeling.

His skin was on hers, his breath on her cheek as he whispered all the things he planned to do to her, as he told her how beautiful she was, how special. She'd never felt so seduced, so aroused or, ultimately, after she'd cried out for the third amazing time, so satisfied.

Later, when they were curled up together, rubbing and stroking lazily, simply for the pleasure of feeling naked skin against naked skin, he said, "Stay tonight?"

"You promised we wouldn't have sex," she reminded him, feeling warm and delicious and full of herself. "If I stay over, you'll want sex."

His chuckle rumbled against her. "Right." He kissed her shoulder. "How about I promise to be a perfect gentleman and not make love to you until morning?"

She opened one eye and regarded him. "What time does morning start?"

"At twelve-oh-one."

She squinted at the clock. "That's three minutes from now."

He nipped her shoulder playfully. "I know. It's going to kill me to wait."

His hand snuck up to her breast and started to play. "What are you doing? It's not morning yet."

"This is foreplay. I didn't promise no foreplay."

"You have to set your alarm for six."

He groaned and did as she asked. Not that either of them got much sleep.

When the alarm went off, she was curled, Nathan's body spooned behind her, his hand on her breast in sleep. She picked up his hand, kissed the chef-knife scar and the soft pink of an old burn. Yep, she thought, thinking of Melissa Tong's recommendation. He really does have amazing hands.

18

As Dennis approached his office he heard an odd sound. Not until he entered did he realize it was Camilla Leeson. And she was singing. Not well and not loud, but he recognized "Banana Pancakes" by Jack Johnson.

"'Banana Pancakes'?" he asked, wondering what had got into his formerly staid associate. She looked heavy eyed, satisfied and altogether smug.

"Oh," she said, startled. "I didn't realize I was singing aloud. I had some, um, banana pancakes. For breakfast."

He raised an eyebrow, letting her know he didn't think she'd run into IHOP on the way to work, and she blushed. Between Mercedes's makeover and whoever was making her breakfast, overnight Camilla had turned into a hottie.

And she was obviously getting some pretty hot sex. Good for her. That only made him miss all the more what he'd had going on with Mercedes. And which now appeared to be going nowhere at all. He'd be damned if he'd call her. He'd offered her love and she'd countered with casual sex.

For a guy who'd always had a very healthy respect for casual sex, he couldn't believe how angry it had made him.

But this thing of hers, fear of commitment, fear of love, whatever it was, was hers to sort out. He needed to give her some time to accept her feelings and him some time to get over his anger at having love thrown back at him like a dirty sock.

"How was your weekend?" Camilla asked him.

He shrugged. "I played squash a couple of times and went for dinner at a golf club thing with my parents." And didn't he sound like a winner?

Dennis was already feeling irritable, and he knew Mercedes was the source. How could she push him away all the time? He loved her and she loved him. What was so difficult about that?

How did you show the most stubborn woman in California that you loved her? How did you show her that you were the kind who committed? He didn't have a crystal ball. Who did? Maybe ultimately they wouldn't make it. Yet it would be cowardly not to try.

"How about you? How was your weekend?" Not that he needed to ask. The first blush of a hot romance was all over Camilla. He only hoped it would last, he thought sourly. He didn't have time for a brokenhearted associate.

Luckily, she didn't waste a lot of time telling him every detail of her weekend. She just said, "I had a good one. Very relaxing."

"Great."

She tapped a finger to a phone message she was leaving on his desk. "Nigel called. There's a problem with the financing on the spa deal."

"What?" He took off his jacket and hung it up. "What problem?"

"The bank manager, the one you figured had a crush on Mercedes?"

"He totally does."

"Well, he took a job in Bermuda. And the new person doesn't seem to have a crush on Mercedes or on her financials."

He cursed softly. Then stomped to the window. "Why does everything always go to hell at once?"

Camilla didn't answer. Probably hadn't even heard him through her postcoital glow.

He turned. "Don't tell Mercedes, okay?"

"Of course not. It's not my place." She looked at him oddly. "She'll have to know."

"I'll get hold of Nigel. We'll make some calls. Before I tell her there's a problem, I'd like to have the solution."

"Right. Um, he said he's already scrambled to find some other financing. That's why he's calling you, because it's not looking good."

"I can't believe this." He'd negotiated with Henry Gorzinsky, once Mercedes had made up her mind that she wanted his location for her second spa. The Polish gentleman had driven all the way to San Francisco to check out Indulge before agreeing—thanks to the potent combination of Mercedes's charm, her business smarts, and Dennis's negotiating skills—to a lower price.

They'd all been so excited. Dennis cursed viciously.

"Nigel said he didn't bother with backup financing. Everything looked fine. He's pretty upset about it."

"Okay. Thanks. Any other disasters today?"

"No, but it's still early."

He picked up the phone and called Nigel and heard again the information Camilla had already relayed.

"I thought the financing was in place."

"It was until the guy handling her file left for Bermuda. Now they're making impossible conditions."

"What conditions?"

"They want a cosigner for the loan."

"That's ridiculous. She's already proven herself."

"I know."

"Have you talked to her?"

"No. I left a message this morning. She hasn't called yet."

How do you show a woman you really love her? He'd asked the question, and here, it seemed, was the answer. You put everything you have on the line for her.

Of course. The solution was right there. "Nigel. I'll cosign the loan."

"What? You're her lawyer."

"No. I'm a lot more than that."

There was a pause, then a startled laugh. "You're not serious. You and Mercedes?"

"I love her." He felt a little foolish, telling Nigel, yet the words felt so right.

"Wow. Well, she's a very nice lady. As your accountant, I have to point out—"

"I know. I don't want to hear it. I've got that money from my grandfather and some property. You know it all better than I do. Put it together, will you?"

"You want more time to think about this?"

"No. Oh, and one more thing, don't say anything to Mercedes."

"But…"

"Really. She needs to stay focused. I don't want her getting bent out of shape over this."

"She's going to find out when she signs the papers."

"I'll tell her. I just want to do it in my own way."

"It's your party."

"I know. Set it up."

"Sure."

He returned to his work, finally putting Mercedes out of his mind.

However, not for long. He went to the coffee room to fill his mug and passed Camilla with a bottle of the mineral water she'd taken to glugging instead of cola, a copy of the *San Francisco Chronicle* in her hand.

She glanced up at him. "Nice picture."

"What?" He felt an unpleasant sinking in the region of his belly.

Sure enough, when she showed him the section where society events were covered, there was the photo of him and Theresa from Saturday night.

"What does this look like to you?"

She glanced at him like he'd taken a squash ball to the head. "It looks like a picture of you, in a tux, with your date, in Vera Wang." She smiled rather smugly. "I admired that dress in a very chichi boutique."

But he wasn't staring at her because she'd guessed the designer. "Why date? Why do you assume date?"

"Because you're standing there with your arm around a woman, and she's resting her head on your shoulder."

"There are four of us in the picture. See? My parents are there, too."

"Yes, so they are. Very cozy." She tapped his arm with the paper, looking, he thought, disappointed in him. "I'd say you're busted."

He groaned. "It wasn't a date."

"Tell that to Mercedes."

"Right. I will. She'll understand what happened. I know she will."

Camilla didn't say a word, merely chugged more water and walked past him.

He stood there, feeling marooned. One of his partners passed him in the corridor and glanced down at the paper held slack in his hands. "Hot date."

"She's not a date. See those other people in the picture?"

The guy's cell rang and all Dennis got was a strange look and a "later" wave of the hand. He stomped into his office and shoved the paper in the trash.

The obvious thing to do was to call Mercedes and check on the level of damage before figuring out the damage control required.

He called her and, surprisingly, got right through. "Hi," he said. "Not with a client?"

"No. I'm between clients. I was reading the paper. Nice picture of you."

"Why don't you let me take you for lunch and explain."

"Sorry, I'm busy for lunch. And you don't have to explain anything. I think our relationship is perfectly clear."

"No, it isn't. At least, not if you're still trying to

pretend it isn't serious. Come on. I haven't seen you in a week. I want to talk to you. And I wasn't 'with' her. You know that. My mother…"

"Why do you escort Theresa to these things if you don't want your mother getting the wrong idea? Have you ever thought about that?"

He opened his mouth to splutter, then shut it again. Damn it, she was right. "I'm sorry," he heard himself say. "You're right. I need to tell them I won't be escorting Theresa anymore."

"Whatever. I've got to go."

Oh, great, he thought. Mercedes was right. He loved her and he needed to make it clear to his family, not only that he had no future with Theresa, but also, he realized with a flash of insight, that he wasn't going into politics.

He felt as though a weight had slipped off his shoulders. Then he called his mother.

MERCEDES ESCORTED CAMILLA to the booty-call meeting for the second Monday in a row. Her protégé was looking even hotter that when she'd first had her makeover. Mercedes was outrageously proud of her. The boot passed to Camilla. She hesitated and said, "I think I'll pass."

"Oh, honey," said Milla. "No good? Look, the first dates are tough. You have to keep trying."

"I don't think she had a bad first date," Rose Leung said, studying Camilla.

"No. I didn't," Camilla said, and blushed. "I've had three really, really good dates this week."

"All with the booty-call guy?"

She nodded, the sparkle in her eyes suddenly evident to everyone.

"No way."

"Get out of town."

"On your first try?"

There was general laughter and teasing, which Camilla took in good humor, until Mercedes could see she was starting to get embarrassed. "So she got lucky her first week." Hoots of laughter told her her little pun was well taken. When it was her turn, Mercedes used the gill net approach, coming out with a fistful of cards.

"Hey," Milla said laughing. "One at a time, girl."

"Sorry." She let all but one slip back into the boot. Read the name off the one remaining card. "Lamont Freeman."

"Oh," Tamara said. "I put that one in there. I'm, um, not sure he's right for you."

"Why not?"

She paused.

"Look, the rule is we only put cards in here if we think the men on them are decent."

"He's decent, all right. Real decent. He's African-American, and—"

"So, I've dated black men before."

"That's not it. He's not really a man, more a boy."

"How old is this kid?"

"Twenty-one."

Mercedes flipped the card over, and Lamont's interests turned out to be skateboarding and stock car racing.

"I'm not sure we should even let this guy remain in the boot."

"I like the sound of him," a shy voice said from the corner. The paralegal from four who rarely showed up.

"And how old are you?"

"Twenty-three."

"I'll swap you, then. Who did you get?"

"A doctor. Trey Patterson."

"What do we know about this Trey?"

"Major hottie," Milla said. "I put him in the boot. He's actually an orthopedic surgeon. Performs miracles, making the lame walk, that kind of thing."

"And you and the good doctor aren't together because?"

Milla's positive spin faltered. She shook her head in disbelief. "He voted Republican." No one laughed. They knew Milla.

"Marital stats?"

"Single. No kids. He said he'd been too busy to settle down."

"Deal," said Mercedes holding out her card. "I'll take the trade."

They left the lounge, Mercedes holding the doctor's card in her hand as though it was a ticket to paradise.

"What are you doing with that card?" Camilla asked her.

"You know how the booty-call works."

"That's not what I asked, and you know it. Dennis loves you."

"Dennis has a funny way of showing it."

They'd walked into the spa and Mercedes strode straight through to her office and picked up the phone.

She didn't realize Camilla had followed her until she heard her voice. "Don't call him."

"Mind your own business."

Camilla, who had not only revitalized her looks but also seemed to have developed a pushy personality in the past couple of weeks, disconnected the phone.

"Hey, this is my phone, my office and my spa. Maybe you should get back to your own job."

"Look, I owe you big-time. I'm grateful for all you've done for me. Dennis, too."

Mercedes put down the phone, keeping her irritation on simmer. "Are you going somewhere with this?"

"Yes. When you and Dennis are around each other there's a kind of magic. When two people are totally in love with each other it creates a kind of force field, an energy that surrounds them. I'm telling you, you can feel it when you two are together. It's powerful stuff."

"I think what you noticed was the force field of lust. I'm not going to pretend that Dennis and I don't get some magic happening in bed. That's all."

"You love him."

Mercedes felt a strong urge to break down and cry. She wanted to throw herself on Camilla's expensively and very tastefully clothed shoulder and sob her heart out. Instead she said, "I'm too busy for love."

"I know. It never happens at a convenient moment, does it?"

"What? You're going to tell me that you're in love? In one week?"

"No. No! Maybe."

"Too bad you and Dennis didn't have the brains to

fall for each other. You both seem determined to rush into disaster."

"You are the one who is headed for disaster if you're not careful." Camilla dragged in a breath. "I can't believe I'm doing this. I think you should call your accountant and get the full details on your financing arrangements."

Mercedes lost all interest in the phone, and her brows rose at the sudden change of subject. "What?"

"I can't say more. I can't." And she was gone.

MERCEDES STARED AFTER HER, puzzled. Even on their short acquaintance, she knew Camilla was not the sort of woman to throw out dark hints unless she could back them up.

Nigel had left her a message this morning, and when she'd returned it, several hours later, he'd merely wanted to see if her timing had changed on the financing. At the time, she'd thought it was a completely unnecessary conversation since nothing had changed.

She picked up her phone and called Nigel.

"Nigel," she said, on the assumption that neither of them had time to waste on beating around bushes, "when you called me this morning, was it really about timing?"

He blustered a bit and then said, "What makes you ask?"

She rolled her gaze. "Women's intuition. What's going on?"

"Um, there was a small problem earlier. It's fine now. With Dennis's help, I was able to iron everything out. I didn't need to bother you, after all."

Something about his tone was off. "What problem?"

"The bank vice president we were dealing with took a job in Bermuda."

"Wow," she said, thinking of his pale complexion and red hair. "Hope he packed a lot of sunscreen."

"The point is, Mercedes, that the rest of the bank's management don't feel as comfortable with lending you so much capital. They're asking for a cosigner."

"What? That's ridiculous. They can't—"

"We hadn't signed anything. They can and they did."

"But, what am I supposed to do?" Her brain was whirling in a mixture of anger, panic and disbelief. "Nigel, have you tried—"

"It's okay. I told you the problem is solved."

"How?"

"Dennis is going to cosign the loan."

"Dennis?" she shrieked the word.

"Yes. Is that a problem?"

"Of course it's a problem. When were you planning to tell me?"

"Dennis said he'd tell you himself. I thought, given the nature of your relationship—"

Mercedes jumped to her feet and cursed. "How dare that conniving, controlling *bastardo* do this to me. He wants to own me, control me, he—"

"Hey, whoa. I thought this would be fine by you," Nigel said. "He's putting up his own assets as collateral. Don't you see? He's betting everything he owns on you it making a success. Frankly, I advised him against it."

"He can't, he shouldn't, how dare he—" She clapped a hand over her mouth, her eyes opening wide.

Then she slowly removed her hand. "He believes in me," she whispered.

"He told me he loves you."

"He's been saying that a lot lately. Maybe I should start believing him."

"Well? What do you want me to do?"

"I can't let Dennis do this. I'm happy to gamble with my future, not with his." She let out a puff of air. "Don't do anything yet. Let me think about this. I'll call you back."

Her hand wandered to that chunk of rock on her desk and she touched its cool, rough shape—history, heritage, family legend—she had a lot to live up to. Was she going about it too fast?

_19_

MERCEDES PUT the orthopedic surgeon's business card back on her desk. She'd return it to the boot next week. Or, wait a minute. Rhonda didn't show up at the meeting today. Hmm. Maybe she'd drop the card off with Rose and get some more matchmaking happening for Rhonda, who really deserved somebody who loved her for more than her great dental alignment.

While she spent a few minutes delivering the card and getting Rose to work on putting Rhonda and the good doctor together, she had time to think.

So, the financing was a mess. What did that really mean?

She strolled out and wandered the spa as she did whenever she needed validation that she was on the right track with her career and her dreams. She saw happy women out there. Women having their aches and stresses melted away by trained massage therapists, their faces and bodies cleansed, nourished and rejuvenated by talented aestheticians until they were younger looking and glowing with vitality.

Mercedes wasn't a believer in cosmetic surgery to fight aging, but she was willing to raid nature's pantry to find natural methods of retaining youthful, beautiful skin and helping her clients look and feel better.

There was a hush in the air, a lot like the hush of a contented beehive. There was work being done here, in this female dominated center. Conversations if the client wanted to talk, Zenlike tranquility if she or he didn't.

Over there a couple of young girls and their mothers had come in for manicures. In the waiting area a woman with bruises of tiredness under her eyes and a complexion dull and waxy waited to be transformed. Sure it was frivolous; still she liked to think she was giving busy women a tiny holiday, a small retreat from hectic lives.

And for that she wouldn't apologize.

Walking out front, she saw three booking clerks busy. She knew that it was getting tough to book an appointment without having to wait. Why wouldn't a similar spa in a similar setting be as successful?

No, she decided, walking back to her office, it wasn't too soon to think of expanding. It wasn't too soon at all.

Of course she wouldn't allow Dennis to guarantee her loan. It hadn't taken her more than a moment to realize that he hadn't done it out of any need to control her; he'd done it because he believed in her.

He wanted her to succeed and was pretty much betting his own money to help her do that.

Yes, he was a little arrogant about it, and yes, he should have talked to her instead of offering to be her guarantor without telling her; nevertheless, she didn't think there was any other way he could have announced that he loved her that she would have believed.

She had clients, of course, all afternoon, and she gave them the best of her services because she was a professional. Underneath her quiet movements and soothing tones was a heart that hammered and a pulse that raced.

How had she confused their deep emotional connection with something purely physical? Scariest of all, how had she almost chased him away?

As she smoothed a clay mask on a crepey neck, as she calmed an oily skin with a special tonic, as she peeled away layers of old skin, purified pores of grime and pollution, nourished the deeper, new skin, she accepted that she loved Dennis. Had probably loved him from the first. That, she realized now, was what made her throw things at him and try to chase him out of her life.

Probably it was the same love that had made it easy for her to accept him as her lawyer and so easily let him back into her bed.

Where she'd been so terrified a few months ago, now she felt a warmth flooding her body when she thought of Dennis and what loving him meant. Things would have to change, of course, and if there'd ever been an inconvenient moment for a woman to fall in love it was while she was planning a major business expansion.

All things considered, she decided, she'd rather expand while she had Dennis on her team and loving her, than on her own.

However, she wouldn't be expanding if she couldn't find another financial backer.

THE HAMMERING on Mercedes's door was so persistent she wished she owned a dog. A big, snarling one that would make any intruder think twice.

She peeked out her peephole and then breathed out in relief.

"Dennis," she said, after opening the door. "I can hear you."

She took one look at his face and wished she hadn't opened up. "What is it?"

"I got an e-mail from your finance guy. I will not be required as your guarantor. You've found an alternative."

Her brows drew together. She had a bit of a trigger temper, and she fought not to let his blazing anger spark some foolishness they'd both regret.

"Why don't you come in? I'll make us some tea."

"Tea," he muttered, as though it was the stupidest idea he'd ever heard. He did come in, though, scowled at her and stomped upstairs toward the living room.

"I wish Nigel had let me tell you myself. I was planning…" He'd disappeared and she shook her head. She'd been planning an intimate celebration for the two of them, where she'd tell him her news and finally reveal her love.

She walked up the stairs.

"I haven't thanked you yet for being willing to guarantee that loan personally, it was…amazing of you."

"Not amazing enough. You rejected me pretty quickly. Again." He sat, then stood again almost immediately. "I didn't mean for you to know. I wanted—"

"You wanted to make things easier for me, and believe me I appreciate it—"

"No. That's not it." He thrust his hands in his pockets.

Walked to the gas fireplace, stared into it as though there were flames leaping and he might be taking inspiration from them instead of doing what he was—staring into an empty black grate. "I thought I was only helping you, proving my support. It was more than that. I wanted to be part of it. Part of what means everything to you."

She wanted to say, "You mean everything to me," but he was speaking again to the grate. She felt like pushing the button for flames just so it wouldn't look so odd.

"I love you, Mercedes. I've tried so many times and ways to tell you, and every time you throw it back in my face."

"No, that's not true. Listen, please."

He shook his head. "I can't do this anymore. I hope you'll be amazingly successful." He turned and his smile was full of pain. "I know you will be. I also know I can't make you love me. And I can't stay in your life wishing it could be different."

"You don't understand at all!" she cried. "I do love you."

"Look, you don't have to say that. I'll be fine."

Finally, finally, she'd said the words back to him. Not as she'd planned, over candlelight and champagne and soft music. But wailed across an empty fireplace. And the flat rejection she saw in his face stunned her. Her voice came out a strained whisper. "You don't believe me."

"No."

"I need to explain. I have to tell you who my new backer is."

"Oh, spare me. I don't want to know his name. I don't want to know anything about him."

Irritation spurted. What could you do with such a man in such a temper? "Then why did you come here?"

"I came to say goodbye."

"Without even giving me a chance to explain anything?" Her anger rose like a hurricane, and she itched to throw something.

"There's nothing left to say. You sent me a message that was as clear as it could be."

"You are such an ignorant, stupid *bastardo*."

"I know that one from freshman Spanish. *Gracias*."

"Oooh." She wanted to throw things, to rage and vent, but her heart was breaking and she couldn't find the energy. "Go, then. I don't want you."

"You made that clear," he said sadly.

He walked up to her.

She glared at him.

He kissed her once, hard, and then he turned his back on her and went down the stairs. She stood there for a moment, so stunned at the way the short conversation had gone that she couldn't quite believe it had happened.

Then, if there was any doubt she'd dreamed the last five minutes, the sound of the front door slamming reminded her that it was real.

Dennis was gone.

Dennis was in the mother of all moods, which wasn't improved when Camilla came in late on Monday morning. She was carrying a paper bag and looking sleepy, sexy and very well satisfied. Since he'd had a weekend that was opposite to that in every possible way, he snarled at her. "I hope there's some very strong coffee in that bag, with my name on it."

Camilla blinked at him, her mind obviously still on whoever she'd left in bed. "Of course not. It's my lunch."

"Since when do you brown bag it?"

"Since a five-star chef decided to make lunch for me," she told him.

He scowled. Not that his mood was her fault, or that she could even see him scowl, since he turned and stomped into his office. He had to get Mercedes out of his mind. Lots of guys broke up. Happened all the time. Lots of love affairs ended.

Worst of all, he realized, lots and lots of hearts got broken. His was only one. Trouble was, even though he'd had his shoulder cried on a few times by friends who'd been thrown out by wives or dumped by girl-friends, he'd never understood how much it really hurt. Not until it had happened to him.

He wouldn't think about her. He had gotten over her once. He could do it again.

Except that he'd never recovered the first time, when he hadn't declared his love, when he hadn't put it all on the line. Now that he had, and she'd thrown it all back at him, he knew the wound was deeper and would take a lot longer to heal.

Most of all, he tried not to think of the name on that line of the banking contract. The one the guarantor signed. Where he would have signed if she'd wanted him in her life.

Jealousy was a new emotion for him and one he didn't like. How many times had she warned him about keeping it casual? How many times had she backed off when he'd tried to claim their intimacy was so much more than sexual?

He'd believed a lot of psycho bullshit about her being afraid of falling in love, afraid of losing. Instead she'd been trying to tell him a very simple truth—she didn't love him. Possibly wasn't even seeing him exclusively.

He couldn't go further with that train of thought or he'd want to punch a hole in the window of his office. So he grabbed some work and tried to concentrate.

When Camilla came into his office later that morning, she caught him holding the photograph of him and Mercedes on the boat. He tried to shove it back in his drawer and then realized that would only make him look more sad than he already was.

He glanced up and their gazes met. "Is everything all right?"

"Well, here we are, you flushed with new love and me flushed down the toilet by love."

Her glowingly fresh Mercedes-enhanced brow crinkled. "What are you talking about?"

"She can't even stand the thought of me cosigning a loan for her. That's how much she wants me in her life."

He glanced up. "Don't shut the door. I don't want one of those heart-to-heart, bare-it-all conversations you women are so fond of." He could have saved his breath. The door shut with a decided click, and Camilla returned, sitting in front of his desk as though she were here for legal advice, instead of—he assumed—being about to dispense personal advice to the lovelorn. Something he really didn't need from a twenty-six-year-old associate who, up until a few weeks ago, had had an exclusive and passionate affair going with law texts.

"Did you tell Mercedes how you feel about her?"

"Oh, God. I knew it. Feelings. If I wanted to talk about my feelings I could go to a therapist or join one of those men's encounter groups."

"Talking to me is free and I'm right here. Did you tell her?"

"Of course I did."

"I bet it was when you were having sex."

He gave her his intimidating glare. That move usually worked on opposing counsel, on witnesses and even, on occasion, on annoying cell-phone shouters. Camilla remained unmoved. Nor did she say anything. Of course, she'd had a lot of the same legal training as he had. She waited him out.

And he cracked. "Yes. I told her I loved her while we were having sex. I also showed her I loved her when I agreed to put my name there on that document, the one that would allow her to achieve her dreams. What is that if not a declaration of love?"

"I think it could be misconstrued as a controlling gesture."

That interpretation hadn't occurred to him. "I never meant it that way. I wasn't even going to let her know. That idiot Nigel must have let it slip before I could explain properly."

Camilla's eyes dropped to the pad of paper in her hand. "Nevertheless, all you have to do is explain to her that cosigning her loan was your rather original way of displaying your feelings."

"Right. Thanks, Counselor. I think that having my signature as cosigner replaced with another guy's pretty much explains how much she wanted me to be a part of her life." He scowled at the photo he still held and shoved it back in the drawer.

Camilla looked at him with pity.

"Look, I don't blame her. She tried to tell me she only wanted a casual thing. I was the one who thought we had a future. I was the one who kept pushing her to give us a chance." He shook his head slowly, wondering how he could have believed so intensely that they were meant for each other, how he could have fooled himself that she felt the same way about him, when she'd never confessed to love—except that one time when she'd been mostly asleep. And the last time when she must have been trying to save his feelings.

Camilla was still looking at him with a serious expression. "You need to go and talk to her. You can't give up because she's got another cosigner."

"I did go and talk to her."

"And?"

"And I said some things?"

"Falling on your knees vowing undying devotion? Those kinds of things?"

He felt revolted by the very idea. "No. 'Thanks for not letting me be a part of your life. Have a nice future.' Those kinds of things."

"Did you even ask her who the new silent partner is?"

"No. And I don't want to know." He waved a hand

to shut her up since he could see she was trying to talk. "I'm no more of a sucker for punishment than the next man. She's got somebody else on the string, maybe somebody she trusts and believes in enough to have a chance at happiness. That's great. I'm happy for her," he said, though his tone said the opposite. "I'm taking a break from women for a while."

"Good," said Camilla rising. "You don't deserve a woman like Mercedes."

"Hey," he said, rising also, and speaking to her back as the woman headed for his door. "She's the one who dumped me."

"No, she didn't. The new cosigner is her grandmother." Camilla said then stalked out of his office.

He stood there for a second. Stunned. The rock bottom horror of his own stupidity quivering through him like nausea.

"Camilla," he yelled after a tense second. "Wait!"

20

MERCEDES WAS FURIOUS. Not the cold kind of anger so good for plotting revenge, but the hot, passionate break-everything-in-sight kind. Her hands had been itching all day to break, maim and destroy, and it certainly hadn't helped her mood that instead she'd spent the morning pampering, soothing and improving.

At least it was Monday and she could restock her supply of men. Although they had an unwritten rule about taking one card at a time, she didn't think anyone was going to stop her today. She intended to take home a handful of the suckers. At least one and preferably two men for every day of the upcoming week.

Her heels tapped like machine-gun fire as she stomped her way down the marble hall toward the ladies' lounge. When she got there, she was surprised to see Camilla. "I didn't think you were coming today."

The women in the room all turned to stare at her, and she realized she'd snarled the words. "Sorry," she said, screwing up her face. "I am mad enough to kill that fathead who works in your office. I guess I was taking it out on you."

"No problem," Camilla said. "I think he's a fat-head, too."

She resumed her scowl. And it was a mighty one, so fierce it seemed to pull her whole face earthward. She'd probably throw out a few wrinkles merely from the force of her unhappiness over the weekend. "You heard?"

Camilla was silent for a moment, then nodded.

There was some uncomfortable shuffling as all the women shifted on their seats, nobody making eye contact with her. Then her mood lifted a little. In this room, with these women, it was impossible to stay angry. "You know," she said, "my grandmother always said there are plenty better fish in the sea than ever came out."

Rose Leung smiled at her, the only person other than Camilla brave enough for eye contact. "Okay, spa lady. Since you are obviously single again, why don't you pick first today?"

"Good idea," said Camilla.

"Absolutely," Milla agreed.

"I'm planning to be greedy," she warned them. "I'm taking a fistful of men home with me. Maybe I should go last."

"No. It's okay. You can try them all out for us and report next week."

She grinned suddenly. She was a woman who always rose to meet challenges. A broken heart was going to be tough, but she'd beat it, especially with a bunch of great women on her team.

She flexed her fingers. "Bring on the boot."

There was an air of suppressed excitement in the room and she caught Camilla and Rose exchanging a quick glance. How great that they were all rooting for her. "Rose," she said, "send me some of your luck, some magic. I really need it. The last guy I picked didn't work out so well."

"That bowl is full of magic, Mercedes."

"He'd better not be a loser," she said.

"Hey, don't pick with that attitude. Think positive."

"Okay," she said, her hand hovering above the glass boot. "Let's see, he's going to be a guy I can trust, number one." She thought about what really mattered to her in a man. "And decent. The kind of man who loves you even when you have the flu and you just threw up all over yourself. A man who loves you when you have PMS, feel fat, can't make up your mind what earrings to wear..."

They all nodded.

"He doesn't have to be great looking, you know. Um, steady job. Somebody who isn't going to get all bent out of shape that I'm a success Somebody who will love it and not feel threatened."

"Would you want him to work for you?" Camilla asked, as though this were a real person and she was considering potential candidates to fill the post.

"Maybe. If he wanted to." She grinned. "Wow, wouldn't that be weird?"

"What else?"

She thought about it, all those cards in that boot, so many nice guys in this city and every other city in the country. A lot of them would be good men, decent men, who would all have different things to offer. In the end there was really only one thing that mattered. "He has to love me. Really love me." The sadness that washed over her felt like a cold wave.

"It's time to pick a card," Rose said.

She closed her eyes, wishing for magic, dug deep into the middle of the business cards that represented a good cross section of single, desirable men in the city.

Her hand touched on several and closed on one. She drew it out. Blinked.

It was an elegant rectangle of heavy stock with a bit of gold on it. Expensive. Then so were the fees charged by the law firm of Dunford, Ross and McKay.

J. Dennis McClary was written in simple black print.

She dropped the card hastily. Somebody else must have put his card in there at one time. How bizarre was that.

She drew again. And once more drew Dennis's card.

"What the—?"

This time she drew a fistful of the suckers out and every one of them said J. Dennis McClary—they fanned out in her hand like a kaleidoscope.

There was absolute silence in the lounge. Not the rustle of a paper sack, the scrape of plastic fork on take-out salad tray, not even the sound of breathing. Except from her. Her breath sounded like a strong wind through a narrow tunnel.

When she looked up, every eye was on her. Some sympathetic, some hopeful, some a little damp. Because she didn't know what else to say, she said, "Are you telling me somebody broke the rules and told a man about the sisterhood?"

There was a snort of laughter, and over it she heard Camilla say, "No. I told Dennis I needed every single one of his business cards, his entire stock. I wouldn't tell him why."

"He gave you all his business cards?"

"He'll be scribbling his name and number on scraps of paper for weeks until we can get a new order in."

"He gave you all his cards without even knowing what you were going to do with them?"

"I told him I was going to help him get you back."

She rose, walked over to where Mercedes was sitting with a fistful of Dennis's cards, some of which had slipped to her lap. Camilla squatted so she could look up at Mercedes. She took one of the cards from her lap and held it up. "He is so miserable without you."

Mercedes tried to be a good person and not feel happy that another human being was suffering because of her. Still she wasn't that good a person. "He is?"

"He looks like crap, is obviously not sleeping well, and if you don't take him back so he stops being so miserable and unreasonable, then I'm going to have to look for other work."

"Wow," Mercedes said, "that's pretty serious. I don't want to be responsible for you leaving your job."

"So, call him," Milla piped up.

She glanced at the boot, full almost to overflowing with Dennis's cards. Of course, if she'd looked more closely, she'd have realized these cards all looked the same and were all fresh and new. A burble of foolish laughter rose in her throat.

"That's a lot of business cards."

"We just got new stock last week," Camilla said. Then she touched Mercedes's hand as she rose. "Call him. Please."

She nodded. It was time. It was time to face up to her own fears and foolishness. Sure, it might not work out.

But not to take a chance on forever love just because it might not work out?

That was the action of a coward. And Mercedes was through being a coward at love.

With a lot of giggling and fanfare, the rest of the booty-call girls dumped out Dennis's entire business card collection and hauled out a shopping bag with the real cards. They placed them ceremoniously in the glass boot and she watched for a while as the weekly ritual resumed. There was so much laughter there, so much hope. In the end, this group of smart, successful, wonderful women, all believed in the possibility of love.

Maybe it was time to accept that she had found it.

When Rhonda shook her head and revealed that she was dating the orthopedic surgeon pretty steadily, Mercedes found her moment to slip out, while the squeals and pelted questions for Rhonda covered her exit.

Camilla might have noticed, but she was on her knees trying to stack Dennis's business cards into some kind of order.

Mercedes could have gone to help her. First she had to put her own life in order and she knew that was what Camilla would prefer.

DENNIS PRETENDED he was going over a brief, glancing at his phone every second, willing it to ring. He had his cell out on the desk, too, in easy reach for her call. Camilla had said she'd call.

She had to call.

When he heard a knock on his open door, he glanced up and felt his world shift slightly sideways. Mercedes stood in his doorway. For a second neither of them spoke or moved. She looked as stunning as always, though something was different. It took him a moment to realize that her expression of vulnerability was new.

His heart began to pound.

"Come on in," he said. He thought about adding, "shut the door." For some reason he didn't. Maybe she was going to need an escape route. Or maybe he would.

She walked in, and he wanted to walk around his desk and pull her into his arms and kiss the life out of her. He didn't. This was her show now. He had some things he needed to say, and she looked as though she had some, too. Since she'd come to him, she deserved the lead.

So he sat as still as he could and waited.

"I hope I'm not disturbing you."

"No." Ha, she should check his pulse. He was close to having a stroke.

She smiled.. He caught the quiver beneath the lips she'd painted a bold, I'm-in-charge glossy red.

"I brought you something," she said, and placed a paper bag on his desk.

He stared at it. It was the cousin of the bag she'd so recently given him containing cherries, a bar of chocolate and a candle. His heart sank and his pulse backed way off from stroke danger zone.

Sex toys. If all she had in mind was more games, then he needed to tell her that he was calling a time-out. No, he realized sadly.

He had to admit he'd lost.

Silence lengthened. "Aren't you going to open it?"

"Mercedes, I—"

"Please, Dennis. Just open the bag."

Something—some trembling quality of uncertainty made him comply. He pulled the bag toward him, hearing the crackle of paper and hoping it wasn't the sound of his future crumbling around him.

The object inside was heavy. He opened the bag and looked inside. It looked very much like a rock.

Puzzled, he reached in and pulled the thing out. Yes, in his hands he held a rock.

He'd seen this rock before. On Mercedes's desk in her office. She used it as a paperweight.

"I'm not sure I—"

"It's from my family's property in Guadalajara. When they came to California, my grandparents brought plant cuttings and my grandmother brought this with her." He was watching her face, feeling the rock heavy and warming in his hands as it drew heat from his body. Her eyes were glistening, and as he watched, a single tear spilled over. "This is part of my heritage. It's part of me, where I came from, the soil that nurtured my family." She laughed shakily. "It's a stupid present, to give a person a rock, but I wanted to give you something that was part of me. Part of my history." Another tear spilled. "I want you to be part of my future."

"Every building has a cornerstone," he said, looking at the rock as he might a chunk of diamond. "Maybe your life has one, too."

"You do understand."

"I think so."

She sniffed and pulled a tissue from the box on his desk, then blew her nose.

"You were right about me," she said. "I always think I'm so brave, foolhardy sometimes. I was a coward about love. I thought I wanted to achieve all my dreams by myself. I don't. I want you with me."

She put her hand over the stone he held, so her fingers touched his. "I love you and I want to build our life together."

"I want that, too," he said, and found his voice wasn't quite steady, either.

"I'm not sure if I'll make a very good politician's wife. I will try."

"You won't have to. I'm not going into politics. I made that decision in the last week. I think you're going to need my help in building your empire. If you'll accept it."

"Really?"

He smiled at her. "I believe in you. I love you. We'll figure this out."

"Oh, Dennis." She was around the desk and throwing herself into his arms so fast that the rock fell to his desk with a thud.

Then she was kissing him and he was kissing her, and the future was there, in the passion and the hope and the certainty that whatever happened, they were in this together.

* * * * *

Set in darkness beyond the ordinary world.
Passionate tales of life and death.
With characters' lives ruled by laws the everyday
world can't begin to imagine.

Introducing NOCTURNE, a spine-tingling new line
from Silhouette Books.

The thrills and chills begin with UNFORGIVEN by
Lindsay McKenna.

Plucked from the depths of hell, former military sharp-shooter Reno Manchahi was hired by the government to kill a thief, but he had a mission of his own. Descended from a family of shape-shifters, Reno vowed to get the revenge he'd thirsted for all these years. But his mission went awry when his target turned out to be a powerful seductress, Magdalena Calen Hernandez, who risked everything to battle a potent evil. Suddenly, Reno had to transform himself into a true hero and fight the enemy that threatened them all. He had to become a Warrior for the Light....

Turn the page for a sneak preview of UNFORGIVEN
by Lindsay McKenna.
On sale September 26, wherever books are sold.

Chapter 1

One shot...one kill.

The sixteen-pound sledgehammer came down with such fierce power that the granite boulder shattered instantly. A spray of glittering mica exploded into the air and sparkled momentarily around the man who wielded the tool as if it were a weapon. Sweat ran in rivulets down Reno Manchahi's drawn, intense face. Naked from the waist up, the hot July sun beating down on his back, he hefted the sledgehammer skyward once more. Muscles in his thick forearms leaped and biceps bulged. Even his breath was focused on the boulder. In his mind's eye, he pictured Army General Robert Hampton's fleshy, arrogant fifty-year-old features on the rock's surface. Air exploded from between his lips as he brought the avenging hammer down. The boulder pulverized beneath his funneled hatred.

One shot...one kill...

Nostrils flaring, he inhaled the dank, humid heat and drew it deep into his massive lungs. Revenge allowed Reno to endure his imprisonment at a U.S. Navy brig near San Diego, California. Drops of sweat were flung in all directions as the crack of his sledgehammer claimed a third stone victim. Mouth taut, Reno moved to the next boulder.

The other prisoners in the stone yard gave him a wide berth. They always did. They instinctively felt his simmering hatred, the palpable revenge in his cinnamon-colored eyes, was more than skin-deep.

And they whispered he was different.

Reno enjoyed being a loner for good reason. He came from a medicine family of shape-shifters. But even this secret power had not protected him—or his family. His wife, Ilona, and his three-year-old daughter, Sarah, were dead. Murdered by Army General Hampton in their former home on USMC base in Camp Pendleton, California. Bitterness thrummed through Reno as he savagely pushed the toe of his scarred leather boot against several smaller pieces of gray granite that were in his way.

The sun beat down upon Manchahi's naked shoulders, grown dark red over time, shouting his half-Apache heritage. With his straight black hair grazing his thick shoulders, copper skin and broad face with high cheekbones, everyone knew he was Indian. When he'd first arrived at the brig, some of the prisoners taunted him and called him Geronimo. Something strange happened to Reno during his fight with the name-calling prisoners. Leaning down after he'd won the scuffle, he'd snarled into each of their bloodied faces that if they were going to call him anything, they would call him *gan,* which was the Apache word for *devil.*

His attackers had been shocked by the wounds on their faces, the deep claw marks. Reno recalled doubling his fist as they'd attacked him en masse. In that split second, he'd gone into an altered state of consciousness. In times of danger, he transformed into a jaguar. A deep, growling sound had emitted from his throat as he defended himself in the three-against-one fracas. It all happened so fast that he thought he had imagined it. He'd seen his hands morph into a forearm and paw, claws extended. The slashes left on the three men's faces after the fight told him he'd begun to shape-shift. A fist made bruises and swelling; not four perfect, deep claw marks. Stunned and anxious, he hid the knowledge of what else he was from these prisoners. Reno's only defense was to make all the prisoners so damned scared of him and remain a loner.

Alone. Yeah, he was alone, all right. The steel hammer swept downward with hellish ferocity. As the granite groaned in protest, Reno shut his eyes for just a moment. Sweat dripped off his nose and square chin.

Straightening, he wiped his furrowed, wet brow and looked into the pale blue sky. What got his attention was the startling cry of a red-tailed hawk as it flew over the brig yard. Squinting, he watched the bird. Reno could make out the rust-colored tail on the hawk. As a kid growing up on the Apache reservation in Arizona, Reno knew that all animals that appeared before him were messengers.

Brother, what message do you bring me? Reno knew one had to ask in order to receive. Allowing the sledge-hammer to drop to his side, he concentrated on the hawk who wheeled in tightening circles above him.

Freedom! the hawk cried in return.

Reno shook his head, his black hair moving against his broad, thickset shoulders. *Freedom? No way, Brother. No way.* Figuring that he was making up the hawk's shrill message, Reno turned away. Back to his rocks. Back to picturing Hampton's smug face.

Freedom!

* * * * *

Look for UNFORGIVEN
by Lindsay McKenna,
the spine-tingling launch title
from Silhouette Nocturne™.
Available September 26,
wherever books are sold.

nocturne™

Save $1.⁰⁰ off

your purchase of any Silhouette® Nocturne™ novel.

Receive $1.00 off

any Silhouette® Nocturne™ novel.

Available wherever books are sold, including most bookstores, supermarkets, drugstores and discount stores.

Coupon expires December 1, 2006. Redeemable at participating retail outlets in the U.S. only. Limit one coupon per customer.

RETAILER: Harlequin Enterprises Ltd. will pay the face value of this coupon plus 8¢ if submitted by the customer for this specified product only. Any other use constitutes fraud. Coupon is nonassignable. Void if taxed, prohibited or restricted by law. Void if copied. Consumer must pay for any government taxes. Mail to Harlequin Enterprises Ltd., P.O. Box 880478, El Paso, TX 88588-0478, U.S.A. Cash value 1/100 cents. Limit one coupon per customer. Valid in the U.S. only.

5 65373 00076 2   (8100) 0 11265

SNCOUPUS

nocturne™

Save $1.⁰⁰ off

**your purchase of any
Silhouette® Nocturne™ novel.**

Receive $1.00 off

any Silhouette® Nocturne™ novel.

**Available wherever books are sold, including most
bookstores, supermarkets, drugstores and discount stores.**

Coupon expires December 1, 2006. Redeemable at participating
retail outlets in Canada only. Limit one coupon per customer.

RETAILER: Harlequin Enterprises Limited will pay the face value of this coupon
plus 10.25 cents if submitted by the customer for this specified product only. Any
other use constitutes fraud. Coupon is nonassignable. Void if taxed, prohibited or
restricted by law. Consumer must pay any government taxes. Mail to Harlequin
Enterprises Ltd., P.O. Box 3000, Saint John, New Brunswick E2L 4L3, Canada. Limit
one coupon per customer. Valid in Canada only.

52607136

SNCOUPCDN

SAVE UP TO $30! SIGN UP TODAY!

INSIDE Romance

The complete guide to your favorite
Harlequin®, Silhouette® and Love Inspired® books.

✓ Newsletter ABSOLUTELY FREE! No purchase necessary.

✓ Valuable coupons for future purchases of Harlequin,
  Silhouette and Love Inspired books in every issue!

✓ Special excerpts & previews in each issue. Learn about all
  the hottest titles before they arrive in stores.

✓ No hassle—mailed directly to your door!

✓ Comes complete with a handy shopping checklist
  so you won't miss out on any titles.

- -

SIGN ME UP TO RECEIVE INSIDE ROMANCE ABSOLUTELY FREE

(Please print clearly)

_____
Name

_____
Address

_____
City/Town   State/Province   Zip/Postal Code

(098 KKM EJL9)

Please mail this form to:
In the U.S.A.: Inside Romance, P.O. Box 9057, Buffalo, NY 14269-9057
In Canada: Inside Romance, P.O. Box 622, Fort Erie, ON L2A 5X3
OR visit http://www.eHarlequin.com/insideromance

IRNBPA06R   ® and ™ are trademarks owned and used by the trademark owner and/or its licensee.

If you enjoyed what you just read,
then we've got an offer you can't resist!

Take 2 bestselling love stories FREE!

Plus get a FREE surprise gift!

Clip this page and mail it to Harlequin Reader Service®

IN U.S.A.
3010 Walden Ave.
P.O. Box 1867
Buffalo, N.Y. 14240-1867

IN CANADA
P.O. Box 609
Fort Erie, Ontario
L2A 5X3

YES! Please send me 2 free Harlequin® Blaze™ novels and my free surprise gift. After receiving them, if I don't wish to receive anymore, I can return the shipping statement marked cancel. If I don't cancel, I will receive 6 brand-new novels each month, before they're available in stores! In the U.S.A., bill me at the bargain price of $3.99 plus 25¢ shipping and handling per book and applicable sales tax, if any*. In Canada, bill me at the bargain price of $4.47 plus 25¢ shipping and handling per book and applicable taxes**. That's the complete price and a savings of at least 10% off the cover prices—what a great deal! I understand that accepting the 2 free books and gift places me under no obligation ever to buy any books. I can always return a shipment and cancel at any time. Even if I never buy another book from Harlequin, the 2 free books and gift are mine to keep forever.

151 HDN D7ZZ
351 HDN D72D

Name	(PLEASE PRINT)	
Address	Apt.#	
City	State/Prov.	Zip/Postal Code

Not valid to current Harlequin® Blaze™ subscribers.

Want to try two free books from another series?
Call 1-800-873-8635 or visit www.morefreebooks.com.

* Terms and prices subject to change without notice. Sales tax applicable in N.Y.
** Canadian residents will be charged applicable provincial taxes and GST.
All orders subject to approval. Offer limited to one per household.
® and ™ are registered trademarks owned and used by the trademark owner and/or its licensee.

BLZ05   ©2005 Harlequin Enterprises Limited.

THE PART-TIME WIFE

by *USA TODAY* bestselling author

Maureen Child

Abby Talbot was the belle of Eastwick society;
the perfect hostess and wife. If only her
husband were more attentiive. But when
she sets out to teach him a lesson and files
for divorce, Abby quickly learns her husband's
true identity...and exposes them to scandals
and drama galore!

On sale October 2006 from Silhouette Desire!

*Available wherever books are sold,
including most bookstores, supermarkets,
discount stores and drug stores.*

Visit Silhouette Books at www.eHarlequin.com SDPTW1006

Silhouette
BOMBSHELL™

On their twenty-first birthday,
the Crosse triplets discover
that each of them is destined
to carry their family's legacy
with the dark side.

DARKHEART & CROSSE

A new miniseries
from author

Harper ALLEN

Follow each triplet's story:

Dressed to Slay—October 2006
Unveiled family secrets lead sophisticated
Megan Crosse into the world of
shape-shifters and slayers.

Vampaholic—November 2006
Sexy Kat Crosse fears her dark future as a vampire
until a special encounter reveals her true fate.

Dead Is the New Black—January 2007
Tash Crosse will need to become the strongest
of them all to face a deadly enemy.

Available at your favorite retail outlet.

www.SilhouetteBombshell.com   SBDTS

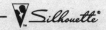

SPECIAL EDITION™

Experience the "magic" of falling in love at Halloween with a new *Holiday Hearts* story!

UNDER HIS SPELL

by KRISTIN HARDY

October 2006

Bad-boy ski racer J. J. Cooper can get any woman he wants—except Lainie Trask. Lainie's grown up with him and vows that nothing he says or does will change her mind. But J.J.'s got his eye on Lainie, and when he moves into her neighborhood and into her life, she finds herself falling under his spell....

Visit Silhouette Books at www.eHarlequin.com   SSEUHS

Those sexy Irishmen are back!

Bestselling author

Kate Hoffmann

is joining the Harlequin Blaze line—and she's
brought her bestselling Temptation miniseries,
THE MIGHTY QUINNS, with her.
Because these guys are definitely Blaze-worthy....

All Quinn males, past and present, know the legend
of the first Mighty Quinn. And they've all been
warned about the family curse—that the only thing
capable of bringing down a Quinn is a woman.
Still, the last three Quinn brothers never guess
that lying low could be so sensually satisfying....

The Mighty Quinns: Marcus, on sale October 2006
The Mighty Quinns: Ian, on sale November 2006
The Mighty Quinns: Declan, on sale December 2006

Don't miss it!

Available wherever Harlequin books are sold.

www.eHarlequin.com   HBMQ1006